Lepke

by

Jack Pearl

Based on the screenplay by

Wesley Lau and Tamar Hoffs

A Warner Bros. Production
Exclusive Worldwide Representatives
Creative Management Associates, Inc.

A POCKET BOOK EDITION published by
Simon & Schuster of Canada, Ltd. • Markham, Ontario, Canada
Registered User of the Trademark

LEPKE

POCKET BOOK edition published May, 1975
2nd printing.........March, 1975

This original POCKET BOOK edition is printed from brand-
new plates made from newly set, clear, easy-to-read type.
POCKET BOOK editions are published by POCKET BOOKS,
a division of Simon & Schuster of Canada, Ltd.,
330 Steelcase Road, Markham, Ontario L3R 2M1.
Trademarks registered in Canada and other countries.

Standard Book Number: 671-78916-3.

Printed in Canada.

LEPKE

Sent to Sing Sing at 16 and raped there, savagely beaten by a convict mob for informing on his molester, he knew all there was to know about uncompromising violence.

Mastermind of 60 gangland slayings, he became the rival of some of the most vicious men that ever lived—like Dutch Schultz, "Legs" Diamond, "Lucky" Luciano and Albert Anastasia.

He made himself undisputed boss of Murder, Inc.—supreme ruler of the underworld.

LEPKE
is an original POCKET BOOK edition.

Books by Jack Pearl

The Crucifixion of Pete McCabe *
Divorce Court #1   Gilchrist vs. Gilchrist: A Question of
    Adultery *
Divorce Court #2   Lazer vs. Lazer: The Black Widow *
Funny Girl *
Lepke *
The Masque of Honor
Stockade *
A Time to Kill . . . a Time to Die
Victims *

* Published by POCKET BOOKS

Lepke

Prologue

Newspaper reporters and photographers jostled each other impatiently in the prison yard as they waited for the infirmary door to open. In the background was a long, black hearse waiting with the same infinite patience reserved for its passengers, past and future.

The chauffeur sat slumped behind the steering wheel reading a New York newspaper. A bold headline took up almost the whole front page:

LEPKE LEAVING OSSINING

He looked up as a clamor erupted from the newsmen. They were coming out now, the draped stretcher flanked by prison guards, followed by the widow, her face hidden behind a black veil. She was supported by a tall, dark man with a grim face.

Hunched over against the force of the wind and the rain and the relentless onslaught of the "ghouls," as Robert Kane called them under his breath, he put one arm protectively around the woman's shoulders and fended off the chorus of questions hurled at her.

"No comment. Mrs. Lepke has nothing to say to you. Now. Never!"

A wry smile touched the lips of the chauffeur as the procession approached the hearse. The cover had been dislodged at the bottom of the stretcher, exposing the feet of the corpse. Shoeless, wearing white socks.

White socks, he mused. A sharpy like him. *He* wouldn't be caught dead in a pair of socks like that!

Chapter
One

Robert Kane would never forget the day he met
Louis Buchalter. It was in the summer of 1912,
shortly after his family had moved to New York's
Lower East Side. A strange, frightening and fasci-
nating neighborhood, like no place he had ever
seen before.

"Teeming," his father had described it. Robert
liked the word; it suggested a colony of busy ants,
a sense of congested, oppressive commotion.

A horse-drawn ice truck stopped in front of a
tenement, holding up the long line of traffic in back
of him. Pushcarts loaded with fruits and vegetables,
one jammed against the other, formed wagon trains
on both sides of the street that stretched on for
blocks.

As soon as the ice man was pushing his way
through the throng of peddlers and pedestrians in-
specting their wares, with a 50-pound block of ice

balanced on one brawny shoulder, his truck was overrun by a flock of human locusts. Kids scrambling for the choice shards of shimmering ice scattered on the tailgate of the wagon and in the dirty street beneath.

It was poetic justice that when Robert spied Louis, he was being chased by a cop. A dark, slim, intense youth who moved with the litheness of a dancer as he waltzed in and out of the pushcarts to the tune of the hurdy-gurdy on the corner. Suddenly he vanished from the sight of the pursuing bluecoat, ducking underneath a cart and slipping into a dark entryway of a tenement.

One danger surmounted as the cop shrugged and walked away. Followed quickly by another as Louis bounded out of the doorway followed by a waddling, screaming, fat lady wielding a broom. He leaped over a gaggle of smaller lads huddled over a marble game and sent one flying. The fat lady bowled over the rest like tenpins. A foot slid over a marble and she went down on her backside with the roar of a wounded hippo.

Louis ducked underneath a cart close to where Robert was leaning against the wall, an admiring spectator at another one of the exciting melodramas he was treated to endlessly on the sidewalks of East New York.

The hurdy-gurdy was playing it:

"East Side . . . West Side . . . All around the town. . . ."

The two boys' eyes met as the cop came running back down the block to see what all the commotion was about.

Louis held up a finger to his lips and Robert squinted up at the blue sky where a homing pigeon was circling for a landing on a roof top.

The fat lady squawked and brandished her fists at the hapless policeman, who tipped his cap and backed away hurriedly. More at ease with young hoodlums than with their victims.

When the coast was clear Louis sauntered out of the hiding place and went over to Robert.

"Thanks."

The new boy beamed with pleasure, nodding mutely. It was the nearest thing to a friendly overture that any of the "old boys" had made to him since his family had moved into the neighborhood. Louis leaned against the wall beside him and took out a pack of cigarettes. He took one and offered the pack to Robert. With trembling fingers he took one and bent to the match the other boy held out. It was the first time in his life he had ever smoked.

Louis could tell. He grinned. "What's your name?"

"Bobby. Bobby Kane," he gasped, his throat constricting on the unaccustomed smoke.

Louis frowned. "What kind of a name is Kane? You must mean Cohen."

Robert was too timid to deny it.

"You know who I am, Cohen?"

Robert nodded vigorously. "Sure. Everybody knows you, Lepke."

Louis Buchalter laughed; he was in a very generous mood. Another day and another boy, such familiarity would have invited a split lip. In the tough, clannish East Side, nicknames such as "Lepke" were restricted jealously for family and close friends.

"You're not afraid of me?"

Robert swallowed hard and shook his head negatively. Scared to death but filled with fierce pride.

Louis studied the new boy with mounting fraternal feeling as the poor boob hacked and wheezed over his virgin cigarette. This one was a virgin in every way, he decided. Without someone to look out for him and set him straight, he'd get eaten alive before the month was out. And here came the guy who would lick his chops over a schlmiehl like Cohen—or was it Kane? He nudged Robert with an elbow.

"Here comes Gurrah. Jake Shapiro," he added, seeing Robert's bewildered expression.

"Why do they call him Gurrah?" Robert asked cautiously.

"You'll see. Watch."

Shapiro was older than the other two boys, the acknowledged leader of the neighborhood gang. A bully with build and disposition of a gorilla. As he swaggered down the block, he grabbed an apple from a pushcart and glowered challengingly at the peddler who shouted after him:

"*Gurrah,* Jake!"

Robert blinked uncomprehendingly.

"It's Yiddish," Louis explained. "Go 'way, Jake. Boy, for a Cohen, you don't know anything."

"Hey, Shapiro Ganov!" he yelled as Jake approached them.

"Gerrarah here!" Jake mimicked the fruit vender.

Louis laughed. "Hi ya, Gurrah!"

As he went by them, Jake turned his head and glanced disdainfully at the new boy.

"Hey, Lepkeleh! Who's that jerk?"

"Don't mind him," Louis told Robert.

Robert was grinning foolishly. What did it matter, calling him a jerk? Gurrah had noticed him!

The victimized vender took two or three steps in the general direction of the departing Gurrah. Pathetic bravado. All of the peddlers in East New York were terrified of Shapiro and his gang.

"Damn Shapiro bum," he muttered self-righteously. "Always stealing from us. Don't his parents feed him?"

"What? From their graves, Max?"

"So why me?" He hit his chest. "Why should I feed him?"

"What else can you do?" Louis said quietly, making a gesture with his hands to indicate benign futility.

The old man shook his head in sad acceptance.

"It's easy for you to say, Lepke. Just the same, someday I'll get the cops and—they'll send the mouser over the water."

"C'mon, Cohen or whatever your name is." Louis started walking with Kane at his heels. As they passed the cart, he deftly snatched an apple from the cart and palmed it until they were a ways down the street.

Nevertheless, Robert Kane was positive that Max had seen him do it and had never uttered a word.

Robert was impressed. Lepke (he felt comfortable with the nickname, as if he had known Louis Buchalter all of his life) was a remarkable and complex personality. Pals with the notorious Gurrah, and yet the pushcart peddlers and merchants seemed to like and respect him as well. Like Max.

"What's over the water?" Robert asked.

Louis jerked his thumb over his shoulder in the general direction of the harbor. "Rikers Island. That's where they send the bad bayo like me."

There was an ambivalence about Louis Buchalter's personality that had been evident since his birth.

Born on the East Side on February 12, 1897, he was an undersized baby with a happy disposition. His father and mother gave him the pet name Label. In Yiddish, Little Louis. With time the pronunciation was bastardized to sound like Lepke. With more time it came to connote something thoroughly foreign to Little Louis. Something monstrous.

The Lepke.

It would strike terror in the hearts of brave men.

In school Louis was a quiet, detached, serious boy who earned passing grades and was a favorite of his teachers. In a section where to be considered a teacher's pet could be the kiss of death, Louis Buchalter's good behavior attracted absolutely no enmity nor resentment from his hoodlum schoolmates. He exuded an air of confidence and authority and fearlessness that made others wary and uncertain in his presence, even one as formidable and avaricious as Jake Shapiro.

Louis, "Lepke" as he was unanimously referred to by then, never involved himself in the traditional school and neighborhood feuds that were a daily distraction from the tedium of slum life with all of its hardships, frustrations and tensions.

Instead he set out to become the arbitrator of the quarrels that went on in school and on the streets. His mind possessed that Solomonic talent for settling issues in such a style that, somehow, each of the opposing parties felt he had come out on top.

His reputation grew with Lepke, and by the time he was in his mid-teens, the older people in the neighborhood were consulting him about their problems. What pushcart vendor had rights to what street and what corners?

The adults were as receptive to his skillful arbitration methods as the young punks, and soon he was known on the East Side as "Judge Lepke."

Ironically, it was his flair for jurisprudence that introduced Lepke to a life of crime.

As Jake Shapiro grew older, he graduated from petty pilfering to feed himself to more sophisticated thievery. Gurrah began to demand protection money from the East Side pushcart owners. If they refused, his gang would upset their carts and kick the fruits and vegetables all over the street. At fifty cents a day per cart, Gurrah was well on his way to becoming a charter member of organized crime.

Faced with this new danger, the vendors put aside their petty intramural squabbles and petitioned Judge Lepke to do something about Gurrah and his strong-arm boys.

With typical unconcern for the murderous reputation of Gurrah ("mad dog" was a favorite description of Jake), Lepke confronted Gurrah alone and on his own turf and told him bluntly to stop terrorizing the pushcart owners.

Totally demoralized by the Lepke mystique, Gurrah began to explain the fine and profitable art of shaking down small businesses, while his followers stood by in open-mouthed incredulity. Lepke listened attentively, and when Gurrah named the amount of "take" the gang had divided in one week, his eyebrows lifted. With more emotion in his voice than anyone could ever remember him evidencing before, he said:

"That much? Well, well, well."

"You could get in on it too, Lepke," Gurrah said slyly.

"Me? Are you crazy? It's not my style to kick over pushcarts and beat up old men."

Gurrah chuckled and laid a big hand on Lepke's knee. "We got the brawns, Lepke. And you got the brains. A real good operation should have both, right?"

"I suppose so," Lepke admitted vaguely. "What do you gorillas need brains for in a crude operation like you run?"

Gurrah's simian brow furrowed. "I'll tell you why. The vendors keep getting harder to handle and they're screaming louder every week. If it keeps up, sure as hell the bulls are going to move in and really flatten us."

"So?"

"The people here trust you—" He let it hang. "—Judge Lepke. They'll do anything you tell 'em. So when they ask you what do they do about the Gurrah, you tell 'em to pay like good little boys and everything will be all right."

When Lepke left the meeting with Gurrah and reported to the anxious pushcart peddlers who had solicited his help, he threw up his hands in resignation.

"It's no use. Nothing can stop them, not even the

police. I wouldn't be surprised if they give the cops a cut to look the other way. Look, you all know the proverb in the Old Testament: 'This too shall pass away.' It won't be long before Jake and his hoods will go on to something bigger. Until then, the best thing to do is to pay."

"Pay," repeated old Max tearfully.

Lepke spread his hands and responded with the phrase that was to become a legendary mark with his victims as he scaled the ladder of crime.

"What else can you do?" His face was impassive.

In all the years he knew Lepke, Robert Kane could count on the fingers of one hand the occasions that he had seen beneath the impassive mask.

Like the afternoon when Louis and Robert were ambling down the street on their way to the Buchalter hardware store.

Robert grabbed the other boy's arm. "Hey! What are all those people doing in front of your house?"

In consternation Louis spit out the apple core he was chewing on and ran down the block. His little sister was at the center of the mob, crying bitterly. Louis grabbed her arms.

"Sarah! Sarah, what is it? What happened?"

The girl threw her arms around him and buried her face against him, sobbing. "Oh, Lepkele. . . . It's papa. . . . He was on the floor."

Louis stopped breathing. "Dead?"

Her loud wailing was answer enough.

"Where's mama?" he asked in a dull voice.

"With papa." A shudder wracked her body. "She said you were the death of him."

Louis recoiled as if she had struck him a physical blow. Shock gave way to anger. He pushed Sarah away and looked around wildly. The horse-drawn city ambulance bearing the body of his father was rumbling over the cobblestones far down the block. Louis ran after it. Ran until his lungs were burning for air and the roaring in his ears drowned out the bedlam of the teeming streets. With a desperate burst of energy, he caught up with the wagon and clutched the tailgate. He clung there with his bare feet dragging across the stones and his cheek pressed to the rough wooden boards. Tears streamed down his cheeks and melted into the dust and dung littering the street.

Chapter
Two

Lepke now was an active and constructive member of the Gurrah mob. The gang was more diversified. With the merchants of the neighborhood resigned to paying their weekly tribute faithfully, the gang went in for robbing jewelry stores and warehouses.

"You're getting good," Gurrah said admiringly one night, watching Lepke smash a hole in a display window and scoop out the loot all in one swift practiced motion.

Lepke smirked.

Gurrah cleared his throat self-importantly. "Few more years and you'll maybe be as good as me."

The smirk exploded into laughter. "I'm better than you ever were, Gurrah, and you know it."

For an instant the older boy's deep-set, mean eyes flashed dangerously. If it had been anyone but Lepke, he would have been lying on his back in the gutter. He lifted a hand, saw the cold challenge in Lepke's eyes and scratched his ear sheepishly.

"Ahhh, you're full of—let's see what you got."
He bent to examine the jewelry in Lepke's hand.

His first armed robbery almost put a premature
end to Lepke's career in crime. Normally when they
hit a warehouse, Gurrah and Lepke would case the
place carefully. Note the time and frequency of
night watchmen making their rounds, the pattern
of police patrols in the street. A shrewd warehouse
guard who did not operate by any predictable
schedule was their undoing.

The two of them were in the act of ransacking
a crate of mens' shoes when a powerful spotlight
blinded them.

"Oh, Jesus! The night watchman!" Gurrah cursed.
As they ducked off behind another tier of crates,
he pulled a gun out of his pocket. "Hey, Lepke,
where's your rod? You got one like I told you,
didn't you?"

"No! I don't want to be caught with a gun."

"You schmuck! Here, better take mine." He tried
to push the revolver into Lepke's unwilling hands.

"No, Gurrah! I told you—"

"Stop or I shoot! Put your hands up!" The watchman was closing in fast.

There was no time for argument. Lepke took
the gun and followed Gurrah down the alleyway
between the stacked crates.

Lepke stumbled and almost fell. "What the hell's
wrong with my feet?" he muttered.

Gurrah was outdistancing him badly. He felt as if he had two left feet. The guard was catching up to him.

"Stop or I'll shoot!"

Lepke stumbled again as the gun cracked and a bullet whistled over his head. He went down to one knee, turned and brought up the gun Gurrah had forced on him. It was reflex action. Self-preservation. He kept squeezing the trigger until the gun jammed. One of the shots winged the man in the arm, but he came on, ready to make the kill, his gun covering the sullen looking youth pinned in the glare of his light.

Slowly Lepke got to his feet and put up his hands.

The night watchman looked up and down. "Okay, wise guy, what did you take?"

Lepke didn't answer, but his eyes cut down to his feet.

The watchman followed his gaze and exclaimed, "I'll be damned!"

Lepke stared at his feet foolishly. He was, indeed, wearing two brand-new, shiny, patent leather shoes. *Left* shoes!

That miscue earned Louis Buchalter his first prison term. Committed to the state prison at Sing Sing, he was assigned to duty in the machine shop. Lacking the skills to operate a lathe, a press or a band saw, he was put on the broom detail. He hated the job, and he hated the other prisoners who constantly referred to him as "kid" or "punk" or other degrading names.

His bitterness and resentment boiled over one day when a man who was shaping legs for chairs on a lathe yelled to him:

"Hey, kid, over here! Sweep up around my feet. On the double!"

Lepke nodded and walked over to him obediently. He wore the expression that had always been so effective in cowing Gurrah. He began to sweep up the sawdust and chips. But then as the prisoner bent over to gauge the bevel of his chair leg, Lepke swung the broom and sent sawdust and shavings flying into his face.

Roaring in pain, he reached out blindly for Lepke, who stood his ground defiantly despite the fact that his adversary was a head taller than himself and twenty pounds heavier.

It was no contest, and all the while that little Lepke was getting the hell beat out of him, the other prisoners went on with their work, pretending that nothing unusual was going on. Enjoying it, really. The kid was not popular with his fellow inmates.

All but one, a big, husky, good-looking man named Al who was one of Lepke's five cell mates. Al was the closest thing to a friend he could claim at Sing Sing. At least he smiled and spoke politely to the youth.

When he judged that Lepke had taken enough

punishment, Al left his machine and stepped between the two battlers.

"That's all, Charley," he told the other man firmly. To Lepke: "Okay, Louis, grab your broom and beat it."

"I'm gonna kill that snotty little bastard!" Charley protested. He tried to get at Lepke again, but Al held him off.

"You calm down, Charley, before the screws see you. You don't want to lose your good time over him, do you?"

"Yeah, well—" He relaxed and began to brush the dust out of his eyes and face with a soiled handkerchief.

The incident bothered Lepke, for some undefinable reason. Every time he came face to face with Al, the big man would beam at him like the rabbi did on the rare occasions when he let himself be dragged off to temple. Like he belonged.

That night Lepke couldn't sleep. He tossed, turned and kicked off his covers. The narrow cot felt like cement. He lay on his back with his hands folded back under his head and stared at the full moon spilling in through the narrow window. Abruptly he started, sensing a presence, yet unseen, moving silently in the darkness. Then a figure materialized out of the shadows and stood at the side of his bed.

"Al!" he whispered in surprise. "What do you—"

"Shhh." The big man held a finger to his lips

and sat down on the bed. Even in the moonlight that silly, simpering smile beamed all over his face; his teeth gleamed like fangs.

Lepke struggled to sit up, but Al's big hand shoved him back gently, held him down. He bent close to Lepke's face and spoke softly.

"I saved your ass today, Louis. You should be grateful. From now on, I'll always take care of you, Louis. You'll see."

What Lepke saw in the moonlight quite literally struck terror to his heart. The prisoners slept in the raw in the heat of summer, and the big man's intentions were only too evident.

Lepke tried to scream, but a big hand clamped over his mouth. He fought with all of his strength, but strong, wiry and tough as he was, he was a boy in the hands of the stocky, hard-muscled man, an ex-stevedore.

Methodically Al rolled him over on his belly and pinned him down beneath his heavy body.

"Oh, Jesus!" Lepke moaned into his pillow. He had heard stories on the outside about things like this. How older prsioners had their "girl friends" in jail.

Gurrah used to joke about it. "Nothing to beat a nice clean boy."

And they would all double up and laugh until their sides ached.

Lepke wasn't laughing now, and never would again at that lousy joke.

He gasped and screamed silently into the pillow as the pain ripped through his body. All of his energy now concentrated on holding back the vomit that churned at the back of his throat.

He was dimly aware of soft, mocking laughter off somewhere in the darkness of the cell. One of his other cell mates really appreciated the joke!

The next day Lepke asked for an audience with the sergeant of the guards. He was escorted to the small, dingy office by two other guards, who kept exchanging winks and grins while Lepke requested a transfer to another section of the prison.

The sergeant listened with a bemused look on his fat, red face and leaned back in his chair. In a mocking tone, he said,

"So you don't like your cell and you don't like your job and you don't like your cell mates. Tough shit, kid!"

"You've got to—"

"Shut up! We don't like smart-ass Jewboys here."

"At least put me in another cell?"

A crafty gleam shone in the sergeant's eyes as he sat up and folded his hands on the desk.

"You want to be treated soft? Okay. Suppose I transfer you? What are you gonna do for me?"

"I'll pay."

"You will, huh?" He glanced up at the other guards. All three wore smug, complacent expressions. "With what?"

Lepke took a deep breath. "I'll work for you."

The sergeant nodded at the guards. "You can go now." To Lepke: "Why don't you sit down, Mr. Buchalter, and we'll have a little talk."

Lepke's role as an informer earned him the transfer he wanted. But the grapevine in stir is both swift and perceptive.

The kid is bad news. A fink. Watch out for him.

After a time it became clear to the inmates in Lepke's section that the warden and the guards knew as much about their secrets as they did. Who had a shiv stashed where. Who stole the butts from the warehouse. Who was planning a break.

Who was the informer?

"Lepke," ruled the kangaroo court to a man.

That afternoon during the exercise period in the prison yard, Lepke was lounging against a wall in the shade watching a softball game. All over the yard prisoners were gathered in cliques of three, four or more. Unobtrusively at first, the groups started to drift in two directions. One converging on Lepke, the other moving to distract the guards to the far end of the area.

Lepke was not aware of what was happening until he spotted an old familiar face in the front rank.

"Al!" he breathed, and the hair at the nape of his neck bristled.

He tried to make a break, but they cut off his escape, a half-circle of men driving him back against the wall.

"Stoolie!" Al hissed, brandishing the jagged lid of an old tin can. The sharp barbs glittered in the sun as it slashed back and forth against Lepke's face. Fists drove into his belly, knocking the wind out of him. Knees brutalized his groin. The last thing he remembered before he passed out were the guards shouting and the rising wail of the siren in the tower.

The incident would set the tone for all the rest of the time Lepke served in prison. An experience that would desensitize and dehumanize and forge the man to the exact degree necessary in order for him to fulfill the destiny that awaited him in the outside world.

Chapter
Three

Lepke was released from prison in the winter of 1922. Instinct took hm back to the old neighborhood in East New York. A fine snow was falling when he came up out of the subway and walked slowly down the street where the family had lived above the Buchalter hardware store. Under one arm he carried a long, oblong package done up in fancy Christmas wrapping. He paced back and forth uncertainly in front of the tenement where he had been born before climbing the steps. He pushed the bell.

The door finally opened and a seedy old woman clutching a sweater tight to her throat squinted out into the snowy twilight.

"Whaddaya want?"

"Mrs. Shea. Remember me?"

She looked him up and down suspiciously. Suddenly recognition flared over her face.

"No, it can't be! Lepkeleh?"

He grinned. "Lepkeleh, that's me."

She flung the door open wide and spread her arms in welcome. "Sure, I remember. How have you been, Lepkeleh?"

He grimaced wryly. "Well, I been away a few years as you know. Just got back to New York today. Have you heard from my ma?"

The women sighed. "Well, gee, not for a few years now. But I heard she and the girls wound up in Colorado. What can I do for you? Look, come inside where it's warm."

He brushed snow off his cheap prison issue overcoat and stepped into the cramped foyer. "I could use a room."

Mrs. Shea shrugged. "The flat your ma used to live in is vacant. If you want it, it's forty a month —in advance."

Lepke smiled. "I'll take it." He took out his wallet and peeled off four tens.

"I'll get you the key." She took the money and went into her apartment at the foot of the staircase. She was right back with the key.

"You know your way."

He chuckled. "I guess so. Thanks. And good night."

Halfway up the rickety steep stairs, he looked back as she called to him.

"Merry Christmas."

"What?"

"Merry Christmas."

"Oh . . . yeah . . . Merry Christmas."

"Who's the nice present for? Your girl?"

He stopped and turned. In a very definite tone he answered, "No."

Lepke wrinkled up his nose distastefully as he made a leisurely tour of the place where he and his sisters had been born and raised.

"What a dump," he murmured. When his father had been alive and the family had been close and happy, it had seemed like a castle to him. Small and shabby, but always clean and neat and in good repair.

Christmas carols filtered through the thin walls from adjacent apartments. He shivered and turned up the collar of his overcoat. The empty apartment had the chill of a tomb. He went into the kitchen and pulled down the stained, tattered shade. He found some old newspapers and egg crates and made a fire in the old potbelly stove around which the family had gathered in bygone days to drink their tea on cold winter mornings. There was a piece of yellow lye soap on the drain board, the kind his mother made herself. He picked it up and held it, a flimsy tie with the past. He shook his head and washed his hands at the sink with cold water. Carefully. Thoroughly.

There was a sense of ritual about his actions now. When the fire was blazing, he slowly removed his clothing, piece by piece, and stuffed each piece in turn into the stove. Savoring the hiss and crackle of the prison clothes burning, shrinking, charring, vanishing into ashes.

Afterward he took a whore's bath in a battered galvanized washtub he found under the sink. He dried himself in front of the potbelly stove; its cast iron sides were glowing cheery red, and the place began to feel warm and homelike once more.

Rubbing his hands together in anticipation, Lepke undid the tinsel cord and gay wrapping paper from the Christmas present. He smiled, recalling what Mrs. Shea had asked him. Was it for his girl?

"Fat chance," he said aloud.

He removed the cover from the box and took out a new tie, a new shirt and a new suit. He fondled the nap of the expensive wool cloth and murmured:

"Merry Christmas, Louis."

When he was dressed he went out into the street. It was bitter cold, but the snow had let up. Two helpful drunks directed him to the neighborhood speakeasy.

A small joint, the room was jammed with holiday celebrants. The dance floor was a mass of writhing, wriggling flesh as sweaty couples made at doing the Charleston. Shimmy and Black Bottom to the time of an off-key piano.

Lepke pushed his way through them on his

way to a table in a remote corner of the barroom. He'd spotted him the moment he came in; who could forget that ugly pan? Jake Shapiro, Gurrah, making out with two girls, or trying at any rate.

Halfway there, he caught Gurrah's eye. The big man's mouth flew open in surprise and Lepke could read his lips:

"Sonofabitch!"

Gurrah shoved the girls away and started toward him.

Lepke felt a tug on his arm. A cute flapper with a short skirt and bobbed hair. She fluttered her eyelashes coyly.

"Hi, handsome. Dance?"

"Later." Lepke left her pouting and kept on walking. They met and regarded each other in silence for a moment. Then the smiles broke through.

Gurrah grabbed Lepke by the shoulders and shook him affectionately. "Well, I'll be damned! If it ain't my old buddy, Lepke. . . . Hey, let me get you a broad."

Lepke chuckled and shook his head. "Same old Gurrah. Thanks, but I'll get my own." His eyes glittered. "You get me some action that's what. I've been waiting a long time."

Gurrah threw his arm around the smaller man's shoulders. "C'mon over and sit down."

Over drinks they reminisced about old times, and

Lepke gave Gurrah a short account of his trials in the state prison. But he was impatient to get done with the past and the present and move on to the future.

"So what have you got in mind for me, Gurrah?"

"Well, how about joining Little Augie?"

"Orgen? What's the angle?"

"Strikebreaking and protection."

Lepke's lip curled. "Like the pushcarts? Fifty cents a week?"

"Come on, Lepke, I'm serious. It pays off good."

Lepke pushed his chair back. "Let's go see Little Augie. Now."

"It's Christmas Eve," Gurrah protested.

"No better time." He got up and Gurrah followed him reluctantly.

In the beginning Augie Orgen congratulated himself on getting such a valuable addition to his mob as Lepke Buchalter. It was not too long, however, before Lepke made it apparent to everyone, notably to Little Augie, that he would rather give than take orders.

His first major challenge to Orgen's authority occurred during a strikebreaking operation at a small Brooklyn factory loft where the garment workers were picketing. Orgen and his mobsters sat in parked cars on the opposite side of the street, watching the picketers marching up and down with their signs that read:

THIS IS A SWEAT SHOP
WE WANT LIVING WAGES
GIVE US WHAT WE DESERVE

"That's our cue, boys," Lepke sang out. "Let's give 'em what they deserve!"

The strikebreakers poured out of their cars waving blackjacks. Lepke and Gurrah were in the front ranks.

"Commie bastard!" Lepke felled a terror-stricken man and looked for his next victim. In minutes the picketers were sprawled on the sidewalk bloody and unconscious or fleeing down the block.

One battered fellow struggled up to a sitting position, and Lepke started for him with the blackjack.

Gurrah grabbed him and pulled him off. "Take it easy, Lepke."

Later Orgen admonished him. "We don't want to kill them, Lepke."

Lepke sneered. "Sez who?" Pointedly he turned to the other men and quipped, "Little Augie is going soft on us, huh?"

There followed a thoughtful silence.

Next time around the mob played the other side of the street. One afternoon Lepke, Gurrah and three others hoods walked into the loft of an East Side dress manufacturer named Stern who had been balking at his protection payments. It was a typical garment factory. Row upon row of tailors hunched over their electric sewing machines. Rotary fans turned slowly in the ceiling.

Stern, working on his statements at a desk on a small dais at the far end of the room, dropped his pencil and got up slowly. The workers eyed the forbidding quintet anxiously, and the rhythm of their sewing slackened perceptibly.

Unhesitatingly Lepke strode over to the switch box on one wall, grabbed the master switch and opened it. The power died.

Gurrah held up his hands. "Okay, boys! We're on strike. Everybody go home."

There were murmurings of confusion and protest from the tailors. Stern came stumbling down from the platform waving his hands.

"Wait! It was all agreed. I gave the raise." He appealed to the shop steward. "Tell these men, Silverman. Everything's settled. Everybody's happy."

Little Augie made his entrance now. "They're not happy, Mr. Stern."

Silverman started to speak, but Gurrah blasted him:

"You heard the man. GO HOME!"

Silverman leaped up and made for the door with the rest of the workers at his heels.

"No, don't go! It's a mistake. "Please!" Stern pleaded with them in desperation. He tried to go after them, but two hoods blocked his way.

Nervously fingering the pins in his vest and the

tape measure slung around his neck, the manufacturer implored Augie,

"Wait— I'll settle it, don't let them go." His voice cracked. "I don't understand. What was the problem, Mr. Orgen? I paid last month."

"You pay *every* week, Mr. Stern. We are your partners, remember?"

Stern was aghast. "Every week! But thirty-five percent is too much. I can't afford it, Mr. Orgen."

To Augie's chagrin, Lepke stepped in front of him. He was soft-spoken and smiling, but the menace in his eyes transfixed the dress manufacturer with fear.

"Mr. Stern, from now on it's going to be fifty percent. And you've *got* to afford it."

Stern kept backing away as Lepke stalked him. "I don't have it! I'm telling you the truth." He was on the edge of hysteria.

"That's too bad, Mr. Stern," Lepke said pleasantly.

Stern had retreated as far as he could. His back was against the open window. Lepke moved in relentlessly, and with one quick motion pushed Stern out of the window.

Ten floors, his screams fading, then cut off abruptly with a dull thud.

"Lepke!" Augie's voice was sharp with anger; he had warned Lepke repeatedly about senseless and unnecessary violence.

Lepke turned to him slowly, the menacing smile

still on his face. His eyes bored into Augie's, and for an instant the gang boss knew the fear that Stern had known, the indefinable malaise of spinelessness which Lepke had inspired in those around him from his boyhood.

"What is it, Augie?"

Augie tore his gaze away from Lepke and growled, "Come on, let's get out of here."

Chapter Four

Ironically the Volstead Act, which prohibited the legal sale of alcoholic beverages in the United States, achieved just the opposite purpose of that for which it was enacted.

The ideal envisioned by its supporters was of a sane, sober, moral America, free of crime and aberations of the flesh and spirit induced by Demon Rum.

All it did accomplish was to goad the American public into an almost militant defiance of the act. To a degree, in fact, that the public became accomplices of the bootleggers who provided them with contraband whiskey. And so with the blessing of their admiring public, the racketeers who controlled the industry were able to accrue huge fortunes and establish the power base that has enabled organized crime in the United States to become the powerful national institution it is today.

At first rival gangs, especially the ethnic groups, battled among themselves for the spoils of narcotics, prostitution and the extortion racket as practiced by Augie Orgen's gang. The Irish, the Jews and the Italians.

The famous St. Valentine's Day Massacre was one of many blood baths that were the product of such rivalry. In a very real sense it was Prohibition that provided the incentive for the various factions to amalgamate or at least arrange an armed truce. The demand for illegal booze was so great that it would take all of gangland's sordid melting pot to satisfy it. That meant working together, and for gang chieftains to sit down together at the conference table at regular intervals to arbitrate disputes, assign territories and explore new opportunities in crime for the future.

By the late twenties it was common to see personalities like Charles "Lucky" Luciano, Meyer Lansky, Buggsy Siegel, Jack "Legs" Diamond and Louis "Lepke" Buchalter dining together at some of Broadway's fanciest night spots.

It was this new spirit of camaraderie among gangland's czars that gave the impetus to Lepke's ambition to take over the Orgen mob.

At one crucial "board meeting" that Luciano attended, Orgen and Lepke became embroiled in a "family" dispute over whether or not to return some protection money to an influential client.

"You want me to do what?" Orgen said incredulously.

"Give the money back," Lepke said flatly.

"Why, for God's sake?"

"Because he's in politics and thick with the unions. We do him a favor, he does us a favor."

Orgen wasn't buying it. "That's a lot of crap! The strike ends tomorrow."

"I think it's a mistake," Lepke maintained.

Orgen pounded the table. "Fifty thousand is a mistake? You're outta your mind, Lepke." He studied him thoughtfully. "How long have you been with me?"

"Five years."

"Getting big for your britches, ain't you?" Orgen glowered.

Lepke stared at him with cold contempt, and it was Orgen who looked away first.

"So, it's settled," he grumbled. "Anybody else got anything to say?"

Luciano's eyes were almost as cold as Lepke's. "I think Lepke's right."

Orgen fought to control his temper. "You're not here to think, Luciano."

He looked to Gurrah and his bodyguard, Jack, for support, but they dropped their eyes and remained silent. Annoyed, he shoved back his chair and got up. "Come on, let's go."

Lepke and Luciano made a show of gathering up their papers as an excuse to remain behind.

Gurrah hesitated at the doorway after the others had left, waiting for his friend Lepke.

Luciano watched Orgen leave and then looked back at Lepke. Pointedly he said, "Now, if he wasn't around. . . ."

Lepke grunted.

Appalled, Gurrah came back into the room. "Jesus! Watch it! You out of your mind or something? You don't talk that way about Little Augie. He'll set you up for a hit."

"Or vice versa," Lepke said. He and Luciano exchanged a meaningful look.

Not long after that meeting Augie Orgen and Legs Diamond were out on the town of an evening. They ended the evening at the Topsy Turvy Club. On the way out they picked up a stylish prostitute made up to look like the flapper of the year and proceeded down the block with her, arm in arm, as they dickered over the price. They paid scant attention to the yellow cab that was following them slowly down the street.

Eventually the deal fell through, and as the whore sashayed away, Orgen turned in disgust and hailed the cab.

"Taxi!" He and Diamond walked over, and Orgen opened the rear door.

Dumbfounded he stared down the muzzle of a Tommy gun cradled in the arms of a smiling Lepke. The driver was Gurrah, disguised in dark glasses and a false mustache.

Alertly Diamond pirouetted to one side as the first blast sent Orgen back against the building. Two more bursts sent him crumpling to the pavement like a sack of flour. Meanwhile Diamond was going for his gun. Methodically Lepke winged off one more shot that hit him in the shoulder and sent him spinning to the pavement.

Pleased with his handiwork, Lepke pulled the door shut and told Gurrah, "Let's go."

As the cab roared away into the night, the rattled doorman who had ducked inside the lobby of the club before the lead began to fly came out cautiously.

Diamond was up on his knees, clutching his wounded shoulder. The doorman cast one fearful look after the speeding cab and decided it was safe to help the stricken man. He put an arm around him and helped him back into the club.

The prostitute, who had ducked into a doorway when the shooting commenced, emerged, looked up and down the still-deserted street and hurried over to the body of Little Augie Organ. Stooping quickly, she slipped her hand inside his blood-soaked jacket and removed his wallet. Tucking it into her purse, she vanished into the darkness again.

Gangland shootings were the grist that best-selling headlines were made of in the twenties and thirties. Little Augie's execution was no exception. And adding to the fanfare and publicity was the fact that another big shot, Jack Diamond, had been a witness to the shooting and had himself been wounded. The other two witnesses got their share of attention too: the doorman at the nightclub and an "unnamed" prostitute who had been with the men when they left the club.

No newspaper reader in the city was more attentive to the situation of the witnesses than Lepke himself.

At the end of the week he invited Gurrah to a private meeting at his apartment overlooking Central Park. It was tastefully appointed right down to the "right" magazines that adorned the coffee table. *Time, The New Yorker* and *The Saturday Evening Post*.

As soon as Gurrah arrived, Lepke pressed him about the witnesses.

The big man was all smiles and confidence. "My pipelines say there's nothing for us to worry about. All of the witnesses got a sudden case of that screwy disease called 'loss of memory.'"

Lepke paced, "It's not good enough."

"What do you mean?"

He stood over Gurrah. "I want them out of the way."

Gurrah shrugged. A few more murders meant nothing to him. "Okay, I'll kill them for you."

"No, I run a clean business from here on. Who's that guy in Brooklyn who takes contracts?"

"Mendy? You want to see him?"

"No!"

"So, I'll see him."

"No. You see Rubin. Tell him to go to Adonis. He'll get the word to Mendy."

"Two contracts?"

"No, three. The girl has to go too."

Mendy Weiss deserved his reputation as the number one hit man for Murder Incorporated.

A few nights later, the doorman of the Topsy Turvy Club opened the door of a taxi, and a young couple got out and went into the club. He paid no attention to the cabby, a squat, swarthy man with a mustache. A pair of predatory eyes watched the doorman in the rear-view mirror as he turned and started back to the main entrance.

With the expertise of a master, Mendy Weiss put the cab into reverse and hit the accelerator hard. The cab jumped the curb and crushed the man against the brick wall. It was speeding far down the street before the first witnesses got to the scene.

Legs Diamond loved the seashore, especially when he was surrounded by pretty girls in revealing bathing suits. He was cavorting with one cutey when a man with a mustache dove in about twenty feet away from them and did not reappear.

Diamond was floating serenely, watching the clouds in the blue sky. He had a brief glimpse of an arm and a hand holding an ice pick emerging from the water alongside him. A blur of motion. He let out a piercing scream as the pick was thurst up to the hilt in his chest.

45

Mendy Weiss surfaced far down the beach and walked nonchalantly up to the boardwalk.

The prostitute who had seen Augie murdered had enjoyed a good week. She was in such a good mood that she decided to make it herself with the john who was making love to her. The sigh of pleasure on her lips became a moan of terror, and her eyes bulged as the ice pick ripped into her throat.

Mendy got up, yawned, and began to dress.

The repercussions were not long in affecting the Lepke mob. Lepke and Gurrah were arrested and charged with the murder of Augie Orgen and with complicity in the murders of the three witnesses. Except that the witnesses were dead. So, predictably, the charges were dismissed for lack of evidence.

Charles Luciano was in court as a witness with two of his bodyguards when the decision was handed down. One of them a good-looking young Turk named Albert Anastasia.

Lepke and Luciano were besieged by reporters as they left the courtroom. The two factions kept a conspicuous distance between them, but they were smiling and affable to the newsmen.

"Is it true that you and Mr. Luciano are splitting up now that Orgen's dead?" a reporter asked Lepke.

"What's to split?"

"Will you take over as head man of your organization, Mr. Lepke?" another scribe asked.

Nodding at Luciano, Lepke told them, "The

board of directors of my corporation will decide that. We're very democratic."

"How do you feel about Mr. Luciano?"

Lepke and Luciano were like Alfonse and Gaston, always bowing and deferring to each other in public.

Lepke answered the question. "I keep telling you. My friend Mr. Luciano and I are in different lines."

Shaking the reporters at last, Lepke and Gurrah hurried away down the corridor toward the main entrance.

To his annoyance, Lepke was stopped by a tall, good-looking young man in a gray suit with a lawyer's briefcase in one hand.

"You wouldn't happen to need a lawyer, would you?"

Lepke, who along with other top mobsters in the state had the best legal talent at his beck and call, almost laughed in the stranger's face.

"A lawyer? Why would I need a lawyer? The charges were dismissed."

The man smiled. "Just thought I'd ask for old times' sake, Louis."

Gurrah was prepared to deal with such effrontery harshly, but Lepke waved him back and peered closely at the man.

"Lepke. The name is Lepke." The face looked— something familiar. "Do we know each other?"

"I'm Robert Kane. We used to live on the same street on the old East Side."

"I don't remember any Kane."

"You used to call me Cohen."

Lepke smiled uncertainly and shook his head. He and Gurrah continued on to the door. Suddenly Lepke turned and gazed back along the corridor. Kane was already walking in the other direction.

He chuckled. "Yeah . . . Cohen."

Chapter
Five

Robert Kane was astonished when, a few days after the meeting at court, Lepke called at his office.

"Louis! This is quite a surprise. Sit down."

Lepke took in the large office, big desk, book-lined walls and the chic secretary. "Very nice. Glad to see you're making out so well."

"Now, what can I do for you?"

"You asked me if I needed a lawyer."

"I was kidding." He grinned. "A man with your business interests must have a team of lawyers."

"Yeah . . . true . . . but I want somebody who'll work for me personally. Give me advice from time to time on personal matters."

"What kind of matters?"

Lepke was amused. "You're careful, huh? Don't worry. I just want a guy I can depend upon to listen to my troubles every now and then. Whatta you say?"

Kane realized that the offer was really an overture of friendship. He knew that if he refused the offer, it would come as a bitter personal rejection to the other man. Tactfully he replied:

"Can I think about it for a while?"

Lepke took out his pocket watch. "How long do you need?"

Kane laughed. "You haven't changed at all, Louis."

"Okay, so it's decided." Lepke stood up and pocketed the watch. "When I need you, you'll hear."

Kane escorted him through the outer office to the door. On the way, he stopped to greet a pretty, petite brunette who was sitting in the waiting room.

"Bernice, you can go right in," he told her.

Lepke looked her up and down admiringly. "I'm impressed with your clients, Kane."

Beatrice smiled at him. "Thank you." As Lepke continued to stare at her, she inquired, "You look at me as if you know me?"

"We're all from the same neighborhood," Kane explained. "Louis, this is Bernice Greenbaum. Bernice, this is Louis Buchalter."

She held out her hand. "Bobby and I have known each other practically all of our lives. How come we never met before?"

Lepke glanced at Kane and straightened his tie. "I was away a lot."

"Oh—at college?"

Kane coughed into his hand.

"Something like that," Lepke said. "Anyway, I got a good education."

Kane took his arm and pulled him toward the door. "So, I'll hear from you." To his secretary: "Miss Tully, you can start to take Mrs. Greenbaum's statement. I'll be with you in a minute, Bernice."

"You called her Mrs. Greenbaum," Lepke said, with his hand on the doorknob. "She's married, right?"

"Louis, I can't discuss my other clients with you."

"All I want to know is if she's married."

Reluctantly Kane admitted, "She's a widow. Her husband died last year. There's some problem with the will."

"I see. A widow. Okay, counselor, thanks for your time."

Gurrah was grumbling when Lepke got into the car. "What took you so long?"

"I met some nice people for a change."

"What makes you think they're so nice?"

"Because they're not like you, shmuck! Let's go, we got business to attend to."

Gurrah started the car and said grimly, "One of these days you're gonna meet one of those nice people, the next day you'll be dead."

Lepke laughed and reached over to pinch his cheek affectionately. "You're stupid—but I love you."

It was noon when Gurrah pulled up in front of the garment factory with a screech of the brakes. Workers eating their lunch on the curb scrambled for safety.

They entered the building and were climbing the stairs to the office when an enormous explosion sounded from the floor above. Plaster and debris showered down on them as they crouched against the wall.

"Someone must have known we were coming," Lepke said.

Gurrah drew his gun and covered his boss as they reached the landing. There was the noise of hurried footsteps coming down the stairs from above. They ducked through a doorway and out of sight just in time, as a troop of men fled past and down the last flight of steps to the ground level. They were shouting back and forth in Italian.

Lepke and Gurrah went up to the factory workroom, where they were stunned by what they saw. Half the machines were wrecked, all the windows were blown out and isolated fires burned all over the smoke-filled room. Out of the smoke staggered the manager of the factory, his head bleeding, his eyes dazed. He threw up his hands when he saw Lepke and Gurrah, then he collapsed on his knees and began to scream hysterically.

"I paid you, didn't I? So why? Is this your protection? I can't pay those wops too." He hit his face with the heel of one hand. "Tomorrow the Irish will come! The hell with all of you! Take everything. Kill me, already!"

Lepke turned angrily to Gurrah. "Let's pay a nice friendly visit to that wop sonofabitch!"

Gurrah's ugly face was morose. "So the Luxkon's moving in on us."

That evening Lepke visited Lucky Luciano in his mob's headquarters at the Royal Hotel. It was obvious to his trained eye that a good many of the people sitting around the large lobby reading papers and performing other idle chores were not hotel guests.

"Lot of our boys here," he said approvingly to Gurrah.

"Take a look."

Lepke told the desk clerk, "Mr. Luciano. He's expecting us."

"Suite eight-oh-four, Mr. Lepke." He dialed the house phone as the two intruders strode purposefully to the elevators.

Two hoods were posted there.

"Ours?" Lepke whispered to Gurrah.

"Lucky's."

On the eighth floor they walked past a crew of carpenters repairing a door.

"Lucky's?" Lepke said out of the side of his mouth.

"Ours."

In the foyer of the suite they were met by three men dressed in suits that seemed too tight for them.

Trigger-happy torpedoes, Lepke appraised them. Tense and poised for action. Trouble all over their faces.

One of them bolted the door. "I'll tell Mr. Luciano you're here, Mr. Lepke."

Lepke and Gurrah did not protest when the other two began to frisk them. But before they were finished, the door leading into the main apartment opened and Luciano was standing in the doorway wearing a big grin.

"Lame brain!" he admonished the hoods. "You don't frisk my guest. Hello, Judge. Come on in."

He led them back to a sitting room, where another member of his staff was sitting with a drink in his hand.

"You boys know Al Anastasia. Have a seat, boys." He turned to the other man. "I like the Judge, Albert, you know that. He always comes up with the right answers."

"Today, I've got questions."

At a signal from Luciano, Anastasia went to the bar to mix drinks for the guests.

Luciano settled back comfortably in his chair. "Here I am, ready to listen."

Lepke wiped a hand across his face. "This is a delicate thing I'm gonna tell you, Charley. So I hope you understand my point of view."

"I'm an understanding man. Go on, I'm listening."

Lepke gave it to him bluntly. "The garment industry is mine, and I wouldn't like it to get away.

Right now I got Amalgamated by the balls. Fifty thousand people, right here in my vest pocket—I own it!"

Luciano looked bored. "So what's your problem? Why are you coming to see me about it?"

"Some of your people are butting in. Naturally I don't like that."

"*My* people? Who do you mean?"

Lepke made it as pleasant as possible. "The old people from the old country. I can understand you like to help them—we do the same." His voice hardened. "But you better teach them U.S. geography! Brooklyn is *my* territory!"

Luciano swung around to Anastasia. "Goddam it, Albert! I thought you were taking care of them."

Anastasia shrugged. "Ahhhhgh. . . ."

Lepke shook a finger at Luciano. "Look, I don't like to tell you how to run your family, you understand?"

"I follow you. Sure, we'll take care of it. But remember, we stay out of your backyard, *you* stay out of our backyard."

"What's that supposed to mean?" Lepke demanded.

"Stay out of the prosties, dope, the waterfront."

Lepke snorted. "I got plenty to keep me busy where I am."

Lepke nodded to Gurrah. "I think it's time we went, Charley." He stood up. "Thanks for the conversation."

"Any time."

When they were gone, Anastasia asked his boss, "Whatta you think?"

Luciano was reasonable. "I think he's got a legit beef. I just don't like the way he did it."

"Smart guys, those kikes. Too smart."

Luciano was unperturbed. "Yeah. So one of these days we'll sit on 'em."

"So what about the greasers who knocked over their joint?"

Luciano mulled it over for a while before he answered. "Like I said, Lepke's got a point. Times change. Somebody said it back in the American Revolution: 'If we don't work together, sure as hell, we're all gonna hang together.' The old greasers will never learn. So, we hit 'em. Hit every goddamn one of 'em!"

For a long time, Luciano had tried to convince the old Mafia bosses to stop the costly mob wars. There was plenty of action for everyone, Italians, Jews and Irish. He envisioned splitting up the rackets into territories.

But the old *Mafioso* with their greasy hair, accents and handlebar mustaches would have none of it. It was an *Italian* family, and no one was going to integrate it!

Big Joe Masseria was the first to go, done in by Joe Adonis in an Italian restaurant while Luciano washed his hands in the men's room and whistled "Happy Days Are Here Again."

LEPKE

Within a matter of hours, across the United States, some forty to sixty Mafia bosses were exterminated in a lightning, synchronized action that would have made General MacArthur envious.

Chapter Six

After their meeting in Robert Kane's office, Lepke and Bernice Greenbaum began to see each other regularly, in spite of Kane's very reasonable opposition.

"I know she's too good for me," Lepke told his friend. "You don't have to say it. But I can't help myself."

Theirs was a clandestine courtship. Lepke didn't want Bernice to find out about his business associates. Bernice didn't want her family to find out about Lepke. Like so many women who become romantically involved with shady men, she had her misgivings, but was able to blind herself to them as long as she didn't know for sure.

One night Lepke was waiting for her in a little Italian restaurant. Lately she had been constantly late for their dates. He gave the strolling accordion player a dollar and told him to haunt the other side of the room. Bernice finally arrived and he stood up as she came to the table, nervously touching his tie.

"Sorry I'm late."

"It's all right."

"Papa always wants to know where I'm going." Her eyes avoided his.

"You tell him?"

"I lie a little."

"He knows about me?"

"He knows I'm seeing someone."

He frowned and shook his head. For a while each of them was lost in his own thoughts. Bernice broke the silence awkwardly.

"You were saying—"

"Huh?" He looked at her startled. Then the two of them began to laugh at the absurdity of the game they were playing.

She put her hand on his. "Really, Louis, what were you thinking about so seriously? Your brow was all furrowed up like an old man's."

"Er . . . I was . . . er . . . I am glad you came."

"That's not what you were thinking. Really."

"No? And what were *you* thinking?"

"Oh, that it's a nice little place."

"Not really," he teased her.

"Not really."

They laughed quietly together and Lepke took her hand and squeezed it. He tensed as a familiar voice sounded over his shoulder.

"Hello, Lepke."

He looked around into the smiling and uncustomarily friendly face of Albert Anastasia.

"Oh, hello, Albert," he said without enthusiasm.

Anastasia appraised Bernice boldly. "Your taste is getting better," he said.

"Thanks." Lepke was cold. "Anything else you want?"

"Introduce me to your charming friend." He made a little bow to Bernice. "I'm Albert Anastasia."

Bernice smiled and nodded. "Nice meeting you, Mr. Anastasia. I was just saying to Louis what a nice place this is."

Anastasia leered at her. "Where the food is good and so are the manners."

Lepke stood up abruptly. "Let's go."

"No, no, be my guests," Anastasia protested. He snapped his fingers at a waiter. "Gino! Wine! Our best," he rattled off in Italian. "And it's on the house."

"We have an appointment, Bernice." He got up, came around and pulled out her chair. Without a glance at Anastasia, he took her arm and propelled her to the door.

"What's the matter, Louis?" she asked in bewilderment. "What did I do?"

"It wasn't you."

"Was it Albert? I don't understand."

"You never know who you bump into these days. I should be more careful."

"Why?"

He ignored her question.

"Never mind, Bernice, how's your boy?"

"David? You know about David?" She blushed.

In those days young widows did not go around advertising the fact that they had children in the early stages of courtship. It tended to scare off prospective husbands.

Lepke smiled and patted her arm. "I think we should get to know each other."

The following Sunday, Gurrah drove Lepke, Bernice and five-year-old David to Coney Island and tailed them at a respectful distance as they went on all the rides and walked along the boardwalk.

That night when he took them home, Lepke told Bernice to send the boy inside. "I have something important to say to you."

When they were alone, he took her hands and looked into her eyes. "Bernice, I love you. And I want to marry you."

Tears filled up in her eyes and her mouth trembled. "Oh, Louis . . . I . . . I . . ."

"Just say 'yes,' "

"I can't."

He put a finger under her chin and tilted it up so that she had to look into his eyes. "You don't love me?"

She shook her head. "That's not it at all."

"Then you do love me."

She nodded with the salty tears streaking down her cheeks. "I do love you."

"Then it's settled." He put his arms around her and kissed her tenderly.

He was wrong about one thing; the issue was far from settled. There was the not-so-small matter of Bernice's father.

The next day he waited for her in the park, feeding the pigeons that flocked around his bench from a bag of crumbs. He glanced at his watch for the tenth time. Late again, as usual. Irritably he scattered the contents of the bag on the ground and got up to pace. His good humor was restored as soon as he spied her coming through the gate. Smiling, he went to meet her. They embraced and then he sat her down on a bench and held her hand.

"Well? What did he say?"

She was not the picture of happiness. "It's so hard, Lou. He's so Orthodox. He wants me to wait a little longer."

He tried to curb his impatience. "Your husband's been dead for over a year now. Isn't that long enough?"

"*I* think so." She watched him closely. "It doesn't matter about David, does it?"

"Of course not. I love him like he was my own son. I should have a son by now."

They walked through the park with their arms

around one another. After a while Lepke asked her about something that had been preying on his mind ever since the day he had met her in Kane's office.

"Bernice. . . . You ever know anyone who's been over the water?"

"You mean in Europe? Sure."

"No, no, not that. . . . Forget it."

She stopped walking and turned to face him. "What *do* you mean, Louis?"

"Prison," he said flatly.

She looked away, off into the distance. "Lou, everyone has a past. I thought we were planning our future." She gave him an affectionate hug, then drew back. He had never seen her look so determined."

"There's only one way to do it, Lou," she said firmly. "You're going to have to come to the apartment and formally ask papa for my hand."

Lepke was stupified. "Ask him for—Bernice, I don't do things that way."

She was adamant. "It's the only way. He's very formal. I told you. Very old world. He'll expect you to ask him if you can marry me."

"God! That'll be worse than talking to Charley Lucky!"

"Who?"

"Nobody. Okay," he gave in. "It's a deal. I'll talk to your father."

She tilted her head, scrutinizing him quizzically.

"I don't know what it is about you I love—but I'm scared of it."

He kissed her and pulled her close to him. "I'm going to take good care of you, don't you worry. I want you to be a queen."

"It's not that, Lou. I'm scared of my own feelings when I'm with you. I think I'd go with you even if pop did say no."

"I wouldn't want you to do that," he said tenderly. "You set it up. Any time he says."

The historic meeting was arranged for an afternoon later that same week. Lepke arrived at the Meyer apartment dressed in his most conservative banker's suit. He was carrying two gift-wrapped packages.

Bernice's mother opened the door to him. He bowed stiffly. "I'm Louis Buchalter."

Flushing, she whipped off her apron and hid it behind her back. A typical Jewish mama, he thought, very much like his own; he repressed a smile.

"Oo—it's you. Please come in. Papa's waiting for you."

"I'll bet he is," he said wryly.

"Pardon?"

"Nothing." He smiled and held out a package in each hand. "And you must be Bernice's beautiful mama. Glad to meet you, mama. This one's for you. This is for David."

Mrs. Meyer beamed at him. "You're just as she said. A gentleman."

She led him into the living room, which was cluttered with too much overstuffed furniture. Bernice's father, a portly man with gray hair and thick glasses, was reading a Yiddish paper. He wore a *yalmulka*.

Not standing up, he put down the paper and indicated for Lepke to sit down. "Take the rocker. It sits very comfortable."

"Thanks." Lepke sat down gingerly and squirmed while the old man looked him over.

"Tonight is Shabbos, Mr. Buchalter."

"I know, sir. I hope you don't mind."

"Mind?" He shrugged. "You're here—so we'll talk. Tell me a little about what you do for a living. My daughter was never able to explain it good for me. She only says you have enough money to support her. Well? Money doesn't grow on trees."

Lepke crossed his legs. "I'm in what you might call—labor relations."

"Might call? *Do* you call it labor relations or *don't* you call it labor relations?"

"Yes, sir. Labor relations."

"Okay. So . . . we got that straight. Which means what exactly?"

"Well, it's a little hard to explain."

"Try me."

Jesus! Lepke thought. The old boy was as sharp as a razor blade. In another part of the apartment, he heard David crying and Bernice and her mother trying to soothe him.

"You mean you don't want to tell me?" Meyer pressed.

Then and there he was saved by the bell. The dinner bell. Mama came to announce: "Papa, you'll talk better on a full stomach. Dinner's ready."

The dining room table was set for a Sabbath feast such as Lepke had not seen for years. Sparkling wine glasses, candles, *challah*, the works. Bernice was standing at her place, very stiff and smiling anxiously. Lepke gave her a reassuring wink and took his place beside her, squeezing her hand.

"Where's David?" he asked her as they sat down.

"Oh, Louis," she said in embarrassment. "I'm so sorry. He's been put to bed without supper because he threw a tantrum over the teddy bear you brought him."

Lepke grinned. "Teddy bears are for babies, right? Guess I've got to learn more about kids. It's not his fault. Let me go to bed without supper and bring him in. Please."

Bernice looked to her father. The old man nodded. "Can't make *Kiddush* without him. Bring him in." While Bernice hurried away to get her son, Meyer confided to Lepke. "He's a good boy. Wait till you see him make *Kiddush* with me. Do you?"

Lepke blinked. "Do I what?"

"Make *Kiddush?*"

Mama saved him once more as she appeared with a bottle of wine for papa to pour. Soon Bernice returned with David, who averted his eyes sheepishly from Lepke.

"I don't know what I was thinking of, getting a teddy bear for a big guy like you. What do you like?"

"Guns!" Meyer said with a vehemence that made Lepke cringe inwardly.

The old man picked up his wine glass and lifted it in a toast. Then he recited the sabbath prayer of thanksgiving.

With mama in the kitchen getting the first course, Lepke took a drink of his wine. Slyly David came up behind him with a toy gun and jammed it into his back.

"Stick 'em up!"

Lepke had all he could do not to obey the natural reflex to hurl himself to one side onto the floor. As it was, he started and spilled wine on the white table cloth. Everyone else thought it was very funny, but truthfully, Lepke's grin was a sickly one.

Mama brought in the *luckshon* soup and Lepke spooned it into his mouth with zest.

"Delicious," he complimented her.

Meyer started to refill Lepke's half-full glass, but Lepke declined.

"I'm not much of a drinker."

67

"No bad habits at all?"

Lepke smiled. "Well, maybe a few."

The smile that Meyer gave him in return made him feel suddenly undressed.

Chapter
Seven

After dinner the two men retired to the parlor. Meyer got right to the point.

"You love my daughter?"

"I love her very much."

"So what more is there? Go ahead, ask me."

"Ask you . . . ?"

"For my daughter's hand in marriage. I like things they should be correct. Kosher. You understand?"

Lepke nodded. "I understand." He coughed in embarrassment and pushed on. "Mr. Meyer . . . I've come to ask you for the hand of your daughter in marriage."

Meyer nodded approvingly. "Okay. Good. Granted."

"You give your consent?" Lepke sounded surprised.

Meyer frowned. "I just said so. You want I should spell it out for you?"

"Thank you."

But Meyer wasn't through with him yet. "Also I want the ceremony in *schul*."

"Where?"

"And you don't know what *schul* is?"

"Well, I—"

Meyer clapped a hand to his head. "*Ochenvey!* A synagogue, young man. Have you never been to one?"

"Sure, when I was—"

Meyer cut him off. "Good. I'd like my daughter to be married according to rabbinical law."

"Of course," Lepke said, slouching weakly in his chair. He had met his match at last.

Meyer beamed at him. "*Mazeltov.*"

The bride and her family arrived at the synagogue long ahead of the groom and his party. Bernice wore a trim suit and a veiled headdress, fitting attire for a widow. She looked happy but nervous. Her father was even more nervous and kept looking at his watch as the wedding guests stirred restlessly in their seats. A mixed bag of the Meyers' neighbors: Jews, Poles, Italians, Lithuanians.

Robert Kane sat alone, a reassuring presence to Bernice. Every time she turned to look at the door,

Robert smiled, and she knew that everything was going to work out right.

The groom's arrival was heralded by a noisy commotion in the street outside the synagogue. Screeching brakes, car doors slamming. It sounded like an invading army, and Kane had to grin as Lepke walked in, flanked and followed by Gurrah and at least fifty more of his hoods. They were all dressed in new suits and they kept glancing uncomfortably around the *schul* as if they expected God to strike them down with a thunderbolt.

Lepke hurried over to Bernice and took her hand.

"I'm sorry, darling."

"It's all right."

It wasn't all right with her father. "You're late," he hissed.

"I'm sorry, sir—there was a—"

"Never mind. Let's get on with it. These men, they're your family?"

"Sort of."

"What do you mean, 'sort of'? Either they are your family or they are not."

The old man was getting under Lepke's hide. "They are—they work with me."

The rabbi came to his rescue. "Are we ready?"

It was a simple ceremony that ended with the traditional breaking of a glass. Gurrah and several of the hoods started at the clatter and put their hands on their guns.

71

The reception went smoothly, although Lepke spent a good deal of time watching his henchmen to make sure they behaved themselves.

When Bernice pulled Lepke onto the dance floor for the first waltz, he was more terrified than he had ever been in his life.

"I've never danced before," he croaked.

She giggled. "Just shut your eyes and hold on, darling."

Gurrah and the other gang members, were bursting with suppressed amusement at the obvious discomfort of their boss. Until other women began to drag them out on the floor.

One incident marred the festivities, for Lepke at least. The unexpected appearance of Lucky Luciano and Albert Anastasia at the door of the hall.

Lepke intercepted them.

At his approach, Anastasia mumbled. "What the hell are we doing here, Lucky?"

Luciano smiled. "I'm here because I wasn't invited. I want to make the little bastard squirm."

"Hello, Charley, Albert," Lepke greeted them coolly.

The two men looked past him as Bernice came up behind her husband.

"How are you, Mrs. Buchalter?" Anastasia inquired politely, just as if he were one of the invited guests.

Bernice was radiant. "I'm marvelous. It's a marvelous day. Won't you come in?"

To Lepke's relief, Robert Kane interrupted them. "Excuse me, I've been looking for you, Bernice—it's our dance."

After Kane had whisked her off, Luciano needled Lepke. "Now that we're all one big happy family in the Syndicate, I kinda hoped I'd get an invite. Whatsa matter, don't you like your Italian pals?"

"I thought a Jewish wedding might bore you," Lepke said archly.

Luciano shrugged. "Could be. Still I figured you could invite the Board of Directors."

"Fine. Come in."

Luciano turned to Anastasia. "Whatta you say, Albert?"

"I'll pass. I gotta date downtown."

Luciano shrugged and spread his hands. "Ahhh, you hear? Albert's got a date downtown. So, if he don't want to come in, I think I'll pass too. Maybe some other time. After you and the missus get settled."

Lepke watched them leave, his face marked by deep concern. Gurrah walked over to him. "Anything wrong, boss?"

Lepke tried to smile without success. "No . . . nothing. Just a little social visit."

Bernice took him by the hand and led him back onto the dance floor. So deep in thought that before he realized it, he was dancing a tango!

Until he met Bernice, Lepke's whole life had

73

been hate and violence, greed and selfishness. His motto:

Look out for Number One.

Now, unaccustomedly, he found himself Number Two on his list of priorities. Bernice and her son, *his* son, meant more to him than did his own life.

Their wedding night was the first tender moment he had experienced in all of his years. The bucket of champagne went untouched as he and Bernice couldn't wait to hold each other in their arms.

She held him with his head cradled on her breasts. It was the only time since she had known him that he seemed to relax. She kissed his ear and whispered,

"You know a secret, Lou? I never thought you'd be willing to wait until tonight." She hugged him. "Do you mind that you won't be able to bring the sheet to your mother?"

"I brought plenty to her when I was a kid. Used to help her hang out the laundry too."

Bernice sighed reminiscently. "My first wedding night, I had to show a little blood."

Inside of him Lepke shuddered. "I wouldn't have wanted to do that to you—I wouldn't want to make a woman bleed."

She bent and peered into his face quizzically. "Lou? You're not afraid of blood, are you?"

His hands moved over her body, caressing, burning with desire. "I don't want to hurt you. Ever."

She stirred against him, responding to his desire.

"I've never been loved before, Lou. Really loved like now."

"I will love you." He kissed her neck with an urgency that was quickly becoming uncontrollable. He pulled the straps of her nightgown down over her shoulders.

Her eyes pleaded with him as he started to get on top of her. "Lou . . . oh, wait . . . please . . . slowly."

For the first time in his life, Lepke exercised restraint; before Bernice he had always taken what he wanted, when he wanted. Making love to his wife, he held back. He seemed to her like the gentlest, most selfless, giving man she had ever known. And the mutual climax, achieved together, was the most wondrous moment either of them had ever experienced.

Holding her close afterward, he whispered, "It's heaven."

She sighed in contentment. "I've never seen you so peaceful before."

"I never thought I could be—unless I was dead."

Chapter
Eight

The joys of his honeymoon were soon overshadowed by the pressures of business for Lepke. Organized crime was singeing under the hot breath of a fire-eating prosecutor by the name of Thomas E. Dewey.

Lucky Luciano called an emergency meeting in 1932 of the mob's Board of Directors to devise a plan to deal with Dewey.

It was a stormy session dominated by the beefy, red-faced Dutch Schultz, the most vocal and violent of the racket bosses. His method of solving the common problem was simple and direct.

"Who the hell does Dewey think he is? Putting the screws on us? Let's kill the sonofabitch!"

Luciano tried to reason with him. "Dutch, you can't kill the D.A., and get away with it."

Anastasia sided with Schultz. "Dirty bastard!

Telling people he's gonna clean up New York. Like we're some kind of shit!"

Luciano wasn't even listening, thinking out loud. "Dewey. . . . There's a man with political ambitions. If there was some way we could use him. . . ."

"He's using us!" Schultz scoffed. "Don't you see that?"

"So, let's buy him."

Jake Gurrah Shapiro shook his head. "You can't buy Dewey. It's been tried."

"Any man can be bought. We just don't know his price yet." Luciano turned to Lepke, who had been unusually silent during the debate. "What do you say, Judge?"

"Let's take a vote," was the reply. Lepke looked around the table. "Who's with Schultz? We hit Dewey."

Three hands went up. Schultz, Anastasia and Gurrah.

Lepke noted the tally. "Three for. All right, who's against?"

Three hands went up. Luciano, Buggsy Siegel and Meyer Lansky.

"It's even," said Luciano. "What about you, Judge? How do you vote?"

"Lepke is always for the hit," Schultz said confidently.

Conscious of all eyes watching him, Lepke decreed: "Killing Dewey is not good for business."

Schultz was outraged. He stood up, kicked over

his chair and shook his fist at the men around the table.

"If you yellow-bellied bastards won't go along with me on this, then I'll do it myself!" He stalked out of the board room.

The remaining bosses contemplated the empty chair in silence. In silent communion. It was Lepke who expressed the common consensus. Schultz had broken the code and there was only one thing to do.

"I move we take steps to protect Dewey."

If Dutch Schultz had any inkling of what his associates planned for him, he did not show it the night he and three bodyguards arrived at one of the favorite mob haunts to eat supper. He wolfed his food, smothered in ketchup, with gusto and joked with his henchmen throughout the meal. In a magnanimous gesture, he tipped the strolling violin player two dollars.

"Hey, there's Mendy Weiss," one hood said.

"Yeah?" Schultz turned and recognized the squat, swarthy man with the bushy eyebrows and mustache. He was eating a steak, cutting small, fastidious bites.

Mendy acknowledged Schultz with a nod and a smile and went on eating. The fiddler was hovering over him.

"Don't be a cheapskate, Mendy," Schultz called to him. He held up a bill, indicating that Mendy should tip the violinist.

Weiss chuckled good naturedly and stood up,

turning to the coat rack behind him. He fished inside his coat for his wallet. Or so Schultz and his men believed. They resumed eating.

Then the mob's number one hit man was facing them with a gun in his hand. There was no time for any of the four in the cramped booth to draw a gun. Calmly Weiss pumped a fusillade of slugs into them until all four were slumped over their plates, blood and gore mixing with the ketchup on the food.

The execution of Dutch Schultz produced the obvious headaches for Lepke, who, as the Schultz mobsters found out, had cast the deciding ballot that doomed their leader. From the other side, the law, captained by D.A. Dewey, intensified its campaign against organized crime. Wherever he went, Lepke developed eyes in the back of his head. He had no intention of blundering into the kind of ambush he had set up for Little Augie, among others.

For a week now he'd been aware that he was being tailed by three men in an anonymous black sedan. It was a cat-and-mouse game that climaxed one evening when Max Rubin paid an unexpected call to his apartment. Rubin was a mob accountant and bag man.

Lepke arrived home late this particular night. Bernice greeted him with a kiss and informed him that Rubin was waiting in the living room.

Lepke was shaken. "Max? Here?"

"Yes, he got here about five minutes ago. Can I get you something to eat?"

"No." He shoved her back in the direction of the kitchen. "Don't disturb us for a few minutes. Please."

Bernice was haughty. "For God's sake, I wouldn't think of it!"

He smiled sheepishly. "I'm sorry." He kissed her cheek and gave her a pat on the rump.

Then, with his anger mounting, he strode into the living room to confront Rubin. A small, pudgy man with frightened eyes, he cringed when he saw Lepke's expression.

"Goddamit! I told you never to come to my home!" he said with controlled fury. "Never!"

"I—I'm sorry, boss," the small man stammered, clutching a fat briefcase to his chest. "But this is an emergency."

"All right! All right! Let's get it over with fast. You weren't followed?"

"No, boss, no. Nobody followed me. I'm positive."

"All right. So what's the big emergency?"

"We need your signature on this contract to make it valid." He fumbled in the briefcase and brought forth a sheaf of papers and a pen.

"Gimme a minute to read it. Then get the hell out of here." He frowned as he leafed through the pages, speed-reading the document.

He glanced up impatiently as Bernice knocked on the door. "I'm making some coffee, Louis."

He grunted. "Max won't have time for coffee."

"Well, it's there if you want it."

Lepke grunted, took the pen from Max and scrawled his signature on the paper.

"There, it's settled. It's a good deal, Max?" In spite of his gruffness with the little accountant, Lepke had a lot of respect for his keen mind and business acumen.

Rubin glowed with pride. "The bakery truckman's local agreed, we get a penny for every loaf of bread they deliver."

"Only a penny?"

"We got seven million people living in this city," Rubin informed him, "and they all eat bread. I figure our cut will come to about thirty thousand a week."

Lepke's strained face broke into a smile. "Well, when you put it that way. . . ." He put an arm around Rubin to escort him to the front door.

At that instant the apartment bell rang. Lepke had a premonition as he heard his wife's excited voice mingling with loud male voices.

Before he could go to her in the hall, Bernice burst into the room, frightened and distraught. At her heels were three men in dark suits and hats. They looked vaguely familiar to him: the men who had been tailing him all week.

Bernice threw herself into his arms. "What's happening, Louis? Who are these men?"

Covering Lepke, Bernice and Rubin with a .38 Special Police Revolver, the tallest man ordered, "All right, put up your hands."

Rubin and Lepke complied.

A second man took out his wallet and showed them his shield. Lepke relaxed. Better the bulls than some of Dutch's friends!

"Detectives without a search warrant," he said ruefully.

Bernice was aghast. "Police? What are they doing here?"

"Who's she?" a detective demanded.

"My wife."

In a more kindly tone, the detective advised her, "You can go to your room, ma'am." He nodded to a small man. "Frisk these guys, Bert."

As his partners frisked Lepke and Rubin, the tall man tried to make Bernice leave, but she was adamant.

"I'm staying with my husband."

"They're clean," Bert announced and put his gun back into the holster.

Lepke was furious. "My lawyers will sue the shit out of you!"

The tall cop smirked. "File a complaint, if you don't like it."

One of his partners had a thought. "Hey, Frank,

what about a vagrancy charge? He might not have money at home."

Bernice sank down on the couch, clasping her throat in disbelief. "Vagrancy. You, Louis? I must be losing my mind."

"Here, try it." He tossed his wallet contemptuously at the detective.

The man took it, rifled through a wad of big bills and threw it back with equal contempt. Without another word, the three turned and left.

Lepke sat down and tried to comfort his wife, who was on the verge of hysteria. She kept shaking her head in bewilderment.

"I don't understand. I just don't—"

He stroked her hair. "Bernice, Bernice, please, it's all right. It's all over now."

Her eyes appealed to him. "But why, Louis?"

"A case of mistaken identity, that's all. I mean, vagrancy. Really!"

She wanted to accept it. Anything but what she had been thinking when the three policemen had invaded her home.

She tried to work up indignation. "Such men! Policemen, they call themselves! They should be punished or reprimanded. Something!"

Lepke exchanged a look with the trembling Rubin. "They will be. I promise you. I'll call my lawyer the first thing in the morning."

Rubin mopped his brow with a handkerchief. "I'll go now. Good night, Mrs. Buchalter."

Lepke followed him into the foyer. His anger at the accountant was rising again. "What the hell was the rush? You coming here tonight. I should really kill you."

Coming from a man like Lepke, it might not be an idle threat. Rubin's face was bloodless as Lepke grabbed his lapels and shoved him against a wall.

"Somebody else was manipulating our bread deal," he said frantically.

"Who?" Lepke's eyes were as cold as a cobra's. "Give me names or shut your mouth."

"I think maybe Joe Rosen. He's just a trucker, but he's big in the union."

"Okay, Max." Lepke released him and his temper cooled. "Joe Rosen. First we get him out of the union. Then you keep an eye on the bastard. And if I should ever forget the name, remind me."

Lepke let him out and closed the door after him. He stood there a minute, mulling over what Rubin had told him. His train of thought was shattered by his wife's voice.

"Lou—these business affairs of yours—are they legal?" Almost as if she were frightened to hear the truth, she added hastily. "You don't have to answer if you don't want to."

He turned slowly and saw her standing in the arch leading into the parlor.

"Why ask it, then?" he said, unsmiling. He went to her.

Trembling, she reached out to him. "Lou, it

doesn't make any difference to me. I want you to know that."

He took her in his arms, kissed her, led her back to the couch. She objected when he tried to force her down.

"No, not now, Lou. David will be home soon."

He laughed. "So, I'll double-lock the door."

Her eyes flashed a warning, and her voice was firm. "No, Lou. Not tonight!"

He let his hands fall to his side in a gesture of resignation. Deep inside he knew he couldn't go on forever, treating Bernice like a child. Pretending, both of them pretending that he was like any other father and husband in the building, going to work in an office or a factory. A normal, productive, wage earner, a pillar of society.

The premonition that had troubled Lepke all week was stronger now.

Chapter Nine

Lepke, true to his word, went to Robert Kane's office the next day, seeking advice. To his astonishment the reception room was stripped of its furniture. He walked through the empty room into Kane's office. Except for a desk and a wastepaper basket, it was bare too.

Kane was standing behind the desk sorting out papers. A few went into his brief case. Most were discarded in the basket. He glanced up when Lepke entered.

"Hello, Louis."

Lepke spread his hand. "You found better offices somewhere?"

"Maybe."

"What's going on?"

"I'm going to Washington, Louis. I'm going to work for the Justice Department."

It was a blow that made Lepke recoil. "You're kidding me."

"I'm serious."

"You're not going to be a cop?"

"Not exactly."

"You *are* gonna be a cop." He shook his head, disbelieving, yet accepting the reality at the back of his mind. He laughed unsteadily. "I hope you don't come running after me."

Kane smiled. "No reason to, Louis—unless you break a federal law. Broken any federal laws lately?"

Lepke studied him as if seeing his old friend for the first time. "I get it, so you're gonna work for J. Edgar Hoover." He paused, seeking the right words to express his feelings. "But *why,* counselor? You got a good practice. Hell, you could make a lot of money. Listen, I can guarantee—"

Kane cut him off with a smile. "Are you trying to bribe me, Louis?"

The humor was lost on Lepke. "I don't like remarks like that, Robert!"

"It was a joke, Louis." He held out his hand. "Well—good-bye for a while."

Lepke ignored the offering, still bridling over Kane's decision to join *their* side. The feds. On the side of the law!

He forced himself to laugh. "Hell, counselor, my businesses, they got nothing to do with the Justice Department."

"I hope not, Louis." Slyly inserted the needle. "How about narcotics?"

Lepka looked shocked. "Narcotics! Shit! I wouldn't touch narcotics with a ten-foot pole! *Good-by!*" He whirled and walked out.

"Take care, Louis," Kane called after him.

Lepke's immediate danger lay not with the F.B.I. but within the ranks of the Syndicate itself. It began when a faction of the Luciano mob, led by Lucky's lieutenant, Anastasia, tried to muscle in on Lepke's slot machine racket.

It was after hours, near dawn, in one of his most lucrative gambling joints. The place was furnished with several poker tables, a crap table, but one-arm bandits dominated the scene along all four walls.

Gross and Schwartz, two of Lepke's mobsters, were counting the previous night's take on one of the poker tables. They were wearing green eye shades and shoulder holsters. They looked up at a knock on the barred door.

Gross got up stiffly and went to the door, opened the peep slot and peered out. The face was strange to him.

"Who's there?" he called.

"Manny sent us to fix your machine."

Gross frowned. "Where's Dan?"

"He's sick. My name's Gino."

Gross hesitated, but finally opened the door. Gino and his partner were friendly, smiling young men with dark hair and dark complexions. Obviously *paisanos*.

Gross led them over to a slot machine on the back wall. "This here is the fouled-up one."

"Yeah, and fix it good this time or tell Manny we'll get new people next time it goes on the fritz," Schwartz put in.

Gross went back to the counting table, but his mind wasn't on the money. He kept watching the two repair men suspiciously. Not that they gave him any excuse to mistrust them. They removed the back of the machine and worked briskly and efficiently for about fifteen minutes. At one point a spring snapped and stung Gino's fingers. He cursed and his partner giggled.

"Sorry, Gino."

"Like shit you are."

Gross began to relax. They were two perfectly normal young workmen.

Except for one thing.

He expressed it to Schwartz after they had left: "Since when is Manny hiring Italians?"

Schwartz shrugged. "One big happy family now, you know that."

The joint filled up early the next evening, mostly regular customers who were familiar with the tribulations that a certain slot machine had presented for over a week now. They avoided it. Until a happy drunk walked in and kept playing the machines at random, moving from one to the other until he came to THE machine. He put his coin in the slot, pulled the lever.

JACKPOT!

The whole place blew up in a gigantic ball of smoke and fire.

The war was on again.

Lepke retaliated swiftly.

Gino, the young hood who had rigged the bomb in the slot machine, was a favorite of Luciano's. When he was married in New Jersey a few weeks later, the church was overflowing with flowers. And in his breast pocket was a fat bonus check from his boss.

Gino and Rosa were a handsome couple as they came running down the steps of the Catholic church after the ceremony. Laughing, shouting, crying relatives deluged them with rice and confetti. The photographer's flash camera blinded them. It was a day of days.

At the bottom of the steps the newlyweds were surrounded by the well-wishers who wanted to kiss the bride and shake the hand of the lucky groom.

As he shook hands with Gino, one man in a dark suit bent close and whispered in his ear. The smile vanished from Gino's face and he glanced uncertainly at Rosa. Wedding day or no wedding day, one did not decline a summons from *him*. Gino whispered to Rosa and then moved off through the crowd after the messenger.

They went around to the side of the church and the man told Gino, "I'll tell him you're here." He hurried into the side door of the church.

Gino licked his lips in anitcipation. Whatever the boss wanted with him, it had to be favorable. After the way he had handled the rigged slot machine, Albert Anastasia had personally taken him out to lunch!

Idly he watched an old-fashioned Italian funeral coming down the side street toward the church. Four pallbearers carrying a coffin, with a small group of musicians in the rear playing the funeral march.

He wondered who the poor devil was destined to go to the grave on this glorious day for himself and Rosa.

It was the last thought in his mind as a high-powered rifle cracked across the street and the slug shattered his heart.

As he fell to the pavement, the funeral procession came abreast of him. It required only seconds for the pallbearers to lower the coffin to the ground —an empty coffin!—and deposit poor Gino's remains in the satin-lined box. The band never missed a beat. On they marched past the church and out of sight.

In front of the church pandemonium reigned as the wedding party searched futilely for the missing bridegroom.

Soon after Gino's body was found, Luciano received an outraged phone call from one of his Jersey compadres. The Jersey mob knew *who* had hit Gino and *why!* Simmering with rage, Luciano summoned Anastasia to his office.

"You stupid sonofabitch! Can't I turn my back for five minutes without you fucking things up? They got Gino. What the hell are you doing, horning in on Lepke's slot machines?"

Anastasia acted surprised that Lepke was offended. "I was only gonna set it up in Jersey, not New York."

The boss pounded both hands on the table. "New York, New Jersey—it's all the same. It belongs to him. Get it into your stupid head. We're part of a syndicate. The Board of Directors decided. We accepted the deal. Now Lepke's sore, goddam sore."

"He's too grabby."

"Look who's talking about grabby. You hear me, Albert, from now on you steer clear of Lepke's territory! Fuck the slot machines! Dope is where the money is, where the future is, and we got that!"

Meanwhile Lepke had been brooding over the Italians knocking off his slot machine parlor. It went on bugging him even after Gino had been rubbed out in retaliation. As Gurrah hinted broadly, maybe his reaction was a convenient excuse to rationalize a thought that had been on his mind for a long time. Luciano's monopoly on the million-dollar drug traffic.

To a word he agreed with the Italian chieftain. "Dope is where the future is," he told Gurrah.

Gurrah disagreed. "I don't like it. You're gonna tangle with Luciano. I mean, real war."

Lepke ridiculed his fears. "Luciano, Luciano, who the shit is Luciano? Some Italian bum, that's all."

Gurrah shook his head. "I can't figure you, Lepke. You're always the guy talking about working together with the other mobs. I mean, we got a real good thing going for us. Why push?"

Lepke shook a finger in his face like a teacher lecturing a pupil. "You don't know what good means. I mean *real* good. Luciano can buy and sell me. All right, it's time I got a share of his gold mine. He tries to horn in on my slot machines; he started it. Now I'm gonna horn in on him!"

Gurrah shook his head broodingly.

"First thing tomorrow, I want you to take a boat to Shanghai."

Gurrah gaped at him as if he were mad. "Shanghai? Me?"

"Yeah, and take Schwartz along with you."

"Where the *hell* is Shanghai?"

"China. Didn't you get any education at all?"

Gurrah groaned and slapped a hand to his forehead. "China. *Oi veh!*"

Chapter
Ten

It was months before Lepke and Gurrah saw each other again, on a bitter cold winter's day. They cleared customs without incident—a key agent was on the mob's payroll—and went directly to an address in Greenwich Village where a rendezvous was to take place.

Gross was waiting for them when they arrived with two large steamer trunks. The trunks were taken up to a one-room unfurnished flat, and Gross and Schwartz stood guard while Gurrah went to contact Lepke.

An hour passed, and Gross was nervous as he paced and kept looking at his watch. A knock on the door sent both men's hands to their guns.

"Who is it?" Gross asked hoarsely.

"It's okay. It's us," Gurrah's gruff voice boomed.

Gross breathed out and unfastened the door chain and opened the door. "It's about time," he grumbled.

Lepke greeted Schwartz and went straight to the trunks resting in the middle of the room. A smile spread over his face as he touched the customs stamps.

"No trouble with our friends in customs?"

"Naw," said Gurrah.

"But they're drooling," Schwartz advised him. "They want a bigger cut."

"They'll get more. It's a cheap investment. Okay, open 'em up."

Gurrah tossed the keys to Schwartz. He unlocked one trunk and swung the two halves apart. One half was the wardrobe section stuffed with suits and jackets. Gurrah removed a sports jacket from a hanger and ripped the lining open with a knife. With a magician's flourish he produced a carefully wrapped package and held it up triumphantly.

"Pure heroin."

Lepke rubbed his hands together in satisfaction. "Pretty good day's work."

He watched with mounting pleasure while Gross and Schwartz methodically stripped the linings out of the rest of the clothing in the trunk and stacked the sacks of heroin on the floor. In the midst of their endeavor there was another knock on the door.

Gross whipped a blanket out of the trunk and covered the heroin. He and Schwartz drew their guns and stood on either side of the door as Gurrah prepared to open it.

"Who's there?"

"Sam Bernstein," was the muffled answer.

Gurrah loked at Lepke for confirmation.

"That's him." Lepke nodded.

Gurrah admitted a little fat man with nervous, darting eyes. He swallowed before he asked, "Mr. Lepke?"

"You got it, Sam."

"Where's the stuff?" Bernstein's eyes widened in awe as Lepke snatched the blanket off the considerable mound of packages. Fingering his double chin, he walked around the pile with the air of a horse trader appraising merchandise. Gingerly he stooped and picked up one package. Lepke and his men watched intently as he tore off a corner, took a pinch of the white powder in his fingers and tasted it. An ecstatic expression confirmed Lepke's expectations.

"First class," the little man said with authority.

"I handle only the best," Lepke said smugly. "How much will it bring?"

Bernstein surveyed the stockpile. "On the *retail* market, Mr. Lepke, you should realize over one million dollars."

Lepke smiled broadly and put an affectionate hand on Gurrah's shoulder. "You know, seeing how the sea air agrees with you, Gurrah, I think you ought to take another boat trip real soon."

Gurrah groaned. "That's ain't funny, Lepke."

Lepke had not meant it as a joke, and not long after the first batch of heroin had been disposed of, he summoned Gurrah into his office and gave him the word.

"China."

"Not again!" The blood drained out of Gurrah's face.

"Like I told you, the fresh sea air will do you good."

"You're trying to kill me. I'd rather you hire Mendy to do it quickly."

"See the same chink. Use the same trunks. It works. Don't change a thing. It's a million bucks."

"Please, Lep—can't I take the train?" Gurrah begged.

"To China?"

Gurrah sat down and buried his face in his hands. Confronted by such abject misery, even Lepke's cold heart melted.

"All right," he said, "We'll send Schwartz and Gross."

Gurrah wore the look of a man reprieved from the electric chair.

Those were the halcyon days for Lepke.

He lived in the style of New York's idle rich. He loved to surprise Bernice with expensive gifts.

One afternoon he suggested the two of them drive over to David's school in Brooklyn Heights and give the boy a ride home.

When they came out of the apartment house, there was a brand-new white Rolls-Royce parked at the curb. A beaming Gurrah held open the door.

"Madame. . . ." Delighted by the excitement in her eyes, he led her over to the car.

"Well, how do you like it?" Gurrah gushed.

Bernice's head was swimming. She could scarcely speak. "Love it—but—but—can we afford it?"

Gurrah and Lepke went into gales of laughter.

Passersby observing their passage through the streets of New York and Brooklyn must have thought they were born to the good life. The lovely woman in furs and diamonds. The stylish young man wearing a London-tailored suit and puffing on a Havana cigar.

When the car drew up in front of Yeshiva of Brooklyn Heights, a crowd of boys led by David descended on them. Lepke leaped out and hoisted his stepson onto the roof of the Rolls.

"What do you think? Should we keep it or give it back to the Indians?" he joked.

Watching him horsing around with the excited boys, Bernice felt a warm glow. It was the side of him that she liked best. The boy exulting over his toys. The other side—she closed her eyes. Bernice didn't want to know what the side of him that she never saw was like.

Lepke had business with the school's head rabbi later on that same week. He and Gurrah were received in the rabbi's study.

"I've brought my accountant, Mr. Shapiro, along. Naturally he keeps track of my charitable donations. I hope you don't mind cash, rabbi?"

The rabbi, a small man who looked older than his years, had stooped shoulders from bearing the burdens and troubles of his flock for so many years.

He smiled and cast his eyes heavenward. "Does *He* mind? His work is done as well with cash."

"Yes, I suppose so." Lepke touched the knot of his tie and gave a high sign to Gurrah.

Clearing his throat self-importantly, Gurrah stepped forward and took a huge clip of bills from his pocket. He wet his fingers and began peeling them off.

"How much, Mr. Buchalter?"

Lepke put his hand over Gurrah's. "Mr. Shapiro— I want to give it all."

Gurrah's voice cracked and he forgot he was supposed to be a C.P.A. "It's ten grand!"

Lepke snatched the roll from him and handed it to the rabbi. "I hope it does a little good, sir."

The rabbi was as shaken as Gurrah by the casual transfer of so much wealth. "I've already ordered the bronze placque with your name on it, Mr. Buchalter."

Lepke smiled and held up a hand. "Rabbi, if you don't mind, I like to keep my contributions anonymous."

Now it was Gurrah's turn to cast his eyes heavenward!

As the rabbi was escorting them along the corridor to the main entrance, he pointed out cracks in the plaster walls; in some places whole chunks were missing.

"You can't imagine how much aggravation we've had with Jenkins Brothers Builders. Look at all the cracks, already. The way they built the Yeshiva it's falling apart. Such cheats."

"What was that name again?" Lepke asked.

"It's those goyish builders. Jenkins."

Lepke turned to Gurrah. "Make a note of that, Mr. Shapiro." And with an intent that was missed by the rabbi: "Take care of them!"

Those were the best times for Lepke, but it was a period that foreshadowed the bad times to come.

Robert Kane returned to New York on a very special assignment for the F.B.I. The Bureau had a fat file on Lucky Luciano, but according to police informers, a new and heavy presence was making itself felt in the illegal heroin traffic. An anonymous "Mr. Big."

Kane and his partner Elson got their first significant lead by working over a bellhop who was pushing horse in a cheap midtown hotel. Not quite as significant to Elson as it was to Kane. When he had taken as much "interrogating" as he could bear, the bellhop finally admitted:

"Okay—okay—so there is a new dealer in town."

"You're damn right!" Elson snapped. "Heroin's dropped to a buck a pop."

"I don't know his name," the boy said. "All I know about him is that he's a Jew."

Elson frowned. "Now, that's a new one. I thought the wops had drugs in their hip pocket."

Kane was silent, averting his face so that Elson would not read his deep concern.

Later the same day he braced himself and paid a visit to the Buchalter's fashionable residence overlooking Central Park.

Bernice couldn't believe her eyes when she opened the door and saw him. Happily she threw her arms around his neck and kissed him.

"Bobby! It's been so long! It's so good to see you."

"It's good to see you too." He hugged her and looked across her shoulder. "Is Louis home?"

Before she could reply, Lepke appeared in the archway. "Who is it, Bea?"

"A surprise."

Lepke's face lit up with genuine pleasure when he saw Kane. He had missed the long talks that he and his "counselor" used to have in the old days. He gave Kane a bear hug.

"If it isn't the Big Man from the F.B.I." He laughed. "When are you gonna take over from Hoover?"

"Hello, Louis." Kane was polite but serious.

Bernice took his arm and tried to pull him into the living room. "Don't stand in the hall. Here, let me take your coat."

Kane held back. "Really, I can't stay, Bea. I was on my way to an appointment, and when I realized

I was in your neighborhood, I thought I'd stop in and say hello."

She patted his arm. "I'm glad you did. Some other time. Some night this week you'll come to supper."

"That would be nice." Kane cut his eyes to Lepke. "Louis, I was hoping I could talk to you for a few minutes. If you have the time, maybe you could walk along. . . ."

Lepke got the message. "Funny, I was just getting ready to take my daily constitutional. Bea, will you bring my coat?"

Bernice stood at the door, looking after them. Long after they were out of sight, she closed the door gently, biting her lower lip. Robert was different somehow. So formal. Like he was making an official visit. She was worried.

They walked through the park in silence for the most part, one or the other offering a strained comment on topics of the day from time to time. Lepke, as was his custom, had stale bread in his overcoat pocket to feed the pigeons. At last he looked at his friend and asked the question that had been on his mind since Robert Kane walked into the apartment.

"All right, Robert, what's the problem?"

Kane squared his shoulders. "Something we heard has me worried."

"Who's *we?*"

"Hoover's in the picture. A pusher dropped your name."

Lepke's expression was impassive. He measured

his opponent—they were on opposite sides now—and decided Kane was bluffing.

"You know me better than that."

Kane wanted to believe him. "Glad to hear it. Because, like I told you once before, Louis, I'd have to come after you if you're into narcotics. And I'd hate it."

Lepke's voice hardened. "Would you really? I think you might enjoy it, Robert."

"I wouldn't. It's not just you who's involved, Louis. Bea and—"

Lepke cut him off angrily. "Take it easy, counselor. Don't grate me. And don't mix my family into this."

"Don't *you* mix your family into it, Louis. Goodby." He did an about-face and walked off, head bent, hands thrust deep into the pockets of his coat.

Lepke shouted after him. "And you can kiss Hoover's ass for me!"

He hurled a handful of bread crumbs into the circle of birds around his feet, and they scattered with squawks of fear and indignation.

Chapter Eleven

From the day Kane warned him, Lepke began girding himself for trouble. And when it came, he was almost relieved. He always preferred to meet life head-on rather than obliquely.

He and Gurrah were in his office when the police cars pulled up in the street below.

Gurrah stood at a window, hands braced on the sill, glowering at them. "Shit! We got company, Lepke. An army of them. Bulls!"

Lepke reclined in the easy chair behind his desk, unperturbed, puffing on his cigar. "Shut up. They've got nothing on us. Not a thing."

Minutes later, a worried-looking bodyguard walked into the office, followed by a natty young man with the look of a lawyer. Lepke knew the type. Like Robert Kane.

"Mr. Lepke?" he asked briskly.

"That's right."

He flashed a badge. "Jack Lansing, United State's Attorney's office. I have a warrant for your arrest."

Gurrah's knees gave way and he sat down on the couch.

Lapke inspected the coal of his cigar. 'Okay, sonny, what's the charge?"

"A federal grand jury has returned two antitrust indictments against you, Mr. Lepke. You're under arrest. If you'll please come with me. . . ."

Lepke smiled and glanced at the frightened Gurrah, mocking him silently. Relief was written all over Jake's ugly face. This was penny ante stuff.

Gurrah gulped. "Antitrust? What's antitrust?"

"A new game these college boys play. And it's a big laugh. Gurrah, call Bernice and tell her I'll be a little late getting home tonight."

A lot later than he imagined. Gurrah and Max Rubin and Allie Tannenbaum, Gurrah's sidekick, kept the vigil at the office late into the night.

When he did arrive finally, he was angrier than any of them had ever seen him. Boiling with rage. Nobody said a word as he flung himself down in the chair behind his desk. He glared at Gurrah, who swallowed hard and mustered the courage to ask:

"You out on bail, boss?"

"Yeah."

"How long before you go to trial?"

"Two weeks."

"Jesus! That ain't very long."

"Long enough." He pounded the desk with a fist.

"Who's the sonofabitch who's singing? Somebody's talking." His voice rose an octave in fury. *"Who's talking?"*

Rubin pulled at his double chin. "It must be Rosen. Joe Rosen. He's been saying all over town he going to see the hotshot D.A.—Dewey."

Lepke frowned. "Who the hell's Joe Rosen? I don't know any Rosen."

"Sure you do," Rubin reminded him. "Remember the Tammany deal? Rosen was that bakery trucker that crossed us. You told me to ease him out. I did and he's sore."

"What's he do now?"

"Runs a little newsstand and candy store over in Bronxville."

Lepke leaned back in his chair and pressed his fingertips together. "Where's Mendy when I need him?"

Tannenbaum got up from his chair in the corner. "I'll get him for you, boss."

"Tannenbaum, you tell Mendy to drop by Rosen's and buy a newspaper. I want Rosen taken care of."

"Boss," Gurrah warned him, "I think we better talk about—"

"Shut up!" Lepke silenced him with a roar. "I want him hit! I want that sonofabitch dead!"

"Boss!" Gurrah pleaded.

Lepke thrust an arm at Gurrah, finger pointing threateningly. "I told you to shut up, Gurrah! You got it, Allie?" Abruptly he slumped in the chair, all of the anger draining out of him. He waved a hand weakly. "Now, get the hell out of here."

Tannenbaum fled the office gratefully. A man like that, all he had to do was to point a finger at you and say: *"Bang, you're dead!"* And you'd better roll over and die!

Reasonable now, Lepke proceeded on to other business. He checked over the papers that Rubin had prepared for him, signed some documents, and asked the accountant, "That matter we were discussing yesterday. That judge?"

"Judge?"

"You know the one. Find a way to get him on our payroll."

"Right." Rubin made a note. "Will that be all, boss?"

"I guess so. I'm bushed." He closed his eyes and wiped his hand over his face as Rubin left.

"Gurrah, there could be other leaks. Find out if anyone else is talking. I don't care who they are. Have them hit."

"Sure, boss, sure, I'll handle it. Just calm yourself down. Get hold of yourself." He took a deep breath before he said what was on his mind, what had worried him earlier. Lepke might cut out his tongue, but it had to be said.

"Boss—don't you know what you just did? You should have let me take care of Rosen. Now Rubin and Tannenbaum can testify you had Rosen hit."

"They wouldn't dare!" But the lines of concern deepened in his weary face.

Gurrah contemplated him silently. The boss was slipping and he didn't know what he could do to help.

On Sunday morning Joe Rosen opened his store at 6:45 a.m. He whistled as he dragged in the bundles of papers that had been delivered overnight. Cut the cords and began arranging them on the racks.

Rosen was dimly aware of a black sedan parking across the street and of the two men getting out of the car. They wore dark coats and their hats were pulled down over their eyes. Customers. He greeted them with a smile as they entered the store. Then his eyes widened in terror as he saw the guns in their hands.

That same day the most famous radio commentator in the United States, Walter Winchell, roasted Lepke in his popular Sunday-morning newscast.

Good morning, Mr. and Mrs. America and all the ships at sea . . . this is Walter Winchell. This morning while most of you were asleep, the city of New York, already incredulous at the news of the release on bail of labor and narcotics racketeer and rumored mastermind of the so-called Brooklyn Murder Incorporated mob, Louis "Lepke" Buchalter, was further outraged by the cold-blooded murder of a law-abiding storekeeper, Joseph Rosen. This brutal killing bore all the earmarks of a Murder Incorporated contract. Isn't it ironic, ladies and gentlemen, that Lepke can only be charged on an inconsequential crime like antitrust and freed on a small fine while his henchmen terrorize our city. When will our law enforcement agencies bring him to justice? Who is responsible? This is Walter Winchell, for September 13, 1936—

In his office Lepke turned off the radio before Winchell's last sentence was complete.

"How come Winchell knows everything almost before it happens?" Gurrah wondered.

"He's clever," Lepke conceded. " I wouldn't mind having him on my payroll."

The door opened and Mendy Weiss strolled into the office. "It's done," he announced.

They looked at him impassively. Gurrah grunted. "We already heard."

In the outer office, Lepke's "staff" was putting in a typical business day. Lounging around with their feet propped up on desks, reading racing forms or girlie magazines. One stood at the water cooler spiking his Dixie paper cup with booze. The timorous entrance of Sam Meyer caused them to look up from their various endeavors with mild curiosity. Meyer was hardly the type of person who visited Buchalter Enterprises.

Meyer regarded the assembly dismally. The looks of this crew confirmed his worst fears about his daughter's husband.

"I got the right place?" he inquired.

"Depends on who you're looking for, pop."

"I'm looking for an office—labor relations office. Louis Buchalter's office."

The hoods exchanged amused looks and winks. One tapped the side of his head, suggesting that the old coot must be off his rocker.

"Okay, who should I say is calling?" one of them asked.

"Tell 'im it's his father."

That bombshell made them sit up and notice.

"You gotta be kidding me, pop," the hood with the phone said.

Meyer was indignant. "Phone it in. Go on, phone it in."

The hood shrugged and pressed the intercom button. "Boss, your old man is here."

His ear rang from the explosion at the other end. He put a hand over the mouthpiece and told Meyer. "His old man's been dead for over twenty years, he says."

"Father-in-law," Meyer spluttered in anger.

"Ahhhh . . . that's different." He spoke into the phone again. "Your father-in-*law* is here, Mr. Buchalter . . . yeah, okay, boss." He hung up. "You can go right in," he said to Meyer.

With a baleful look around the office, Meyer

marched into the inner office. He glowered at Weiss and Gurrah, studied Lepke with only a little less contempt.

"You shoulda told me you were coming," Lepke mumbled self-consciously.

Meyer appraised the lavish room. *"This* is labor relations? I never knew it paid so good. And such a big company without any secretaries."

Lepke's laughter was forced. Bernice's old man had a knack for getting under his skin and putting him on the defensive.

"Why not?" he said lightly. "Like in *schul,* you just have men in the *minyan.* You pray with men. I work with men."

"Comparisons you're making?" He studied Weiss. "So this is a secretary? Hello, secretary."

Weiss smiled coldly.

Lepke was getting annoyed now. "To what do I owe the pleasure of this visit? You got something on your mind?"

Meyer stood up to his full height. "In a manner of speaking I do, Louis. I'm reading the *Tribune* this morning. On page three I see a headline. I read the story. Louis Buchalter, it says, is guilty of breaking the law. What law, I ask myself, could my son-in-law be breaking? It says antitrust or something I don't know about. I read more. A fine—a big fine—the paper says he's gonna have to pay. Not only a fine, but two years in prison. Is that true, Louis?"

"You believe everything you read in the papers?" Lepke asked tersely.

"Why not? I shouldn't? This story I read is not true, you're telling me?"

"It's still gotta be proved."

Meyer lifted his eyebrows. "That makes it not true?"

Lepke turned away from him.

Meyer persisted. "Well, go on—tell me—you know what's true or not true."

Lepke was evasive. "I just said—it's gotta be proved."

Meyer was scornful. "Louis, stop lying to me. I saw it all—outside that door." He pointed to the outer office. Encompassed the sumptuous office with a flourish of his hands. "In here. A gangster you are, Louis—a gangster. Labor relations, you said you were in. Ha! Very funny! And what is this Brooklyn corporation you are in? Winchell said you are in murders."

"And you believe it?" Lepke tried to bluff it out.

"Where there's smoke, there's fire. Louis, it pains me—here, in my heart—to listen to these things about my son-in-law, even if they are lies. But what can I do? I can't do nothing. . . . One thing only I ask. Keep away from me and my wife. My daughter?" He sighed with regret. "She married you, God help her. She's gotta live her own life. I can't tell her what to do. All I ask of you, Louis, is stay outta *my* life!" He turned away contemptuously and walked to the door.

Lepke started after him. "Wait a minute—I'll send you home in my car."

He placed a hand on the old man's arm.

"Pooey! I spit on your car and on you!" Meyer said.

With that he turned and spit into Lepke's face. He marched out of the office proudly, with Gurrah and Weiss slinking out right after him. Leaving Lepke alone in the room, stunned, sickened and frightened. Once things began to go wrong, everything—he didn't want to think about it.

That night Lepke scrubbed his face with a fixation. It seemed he could not wipe away Sam Meyer's spittle. Was it the spit he couldn't wipe clean? Or was it the dirt that the old man had heaped on with his words?

He touched the Italian marble sink, the solid gold faucets. He was a rich and important man. He was also a troubled man.

When he came into the bedroom he told Bernice. "I think we should put David into school out of town. Maybe Miami—he loves the beach."

Bernice put down the Dashiell Hammett mystery she was reading. "Wait till we send him to college."

"He can't stay in this town with all the dirt they're throwing at me," he said tensely. "And maybe you should leave too."

She stared at him with mixed emotions. "And what about you, Louis?"

"What about me?"

"I'm worried about you."

"My lawyers can protect me," he said.

"That's not what I'm worried about."

She held out her arms to him and they embraced with the urgency and fervor of two people who would never see one another again.

Chapter Twelve

When Gross and Schwartz disembarked from the ship that had carried them and their precious cargo all the way around the Cape from China, they went by taxi to the same rendezvous in Greenwich Village that had served as the drop spot the first time Gurrah and Gross had smuggled in heroin from the Far East.

Once they were settled in the apartment with the two steamer trunks, they relaxed with a cigarette and waited for Lepke to arrive. The knock on the door came sooner than they had anticipated.

"That's him," Gross said and headed for the door.

"He's early for a change," Schwartz said.

Gross opened the door and stood there transfixed with fear. He was staring down the barrels of two guns armed wtih silencers. One of the gunmen shoved him back into the room.

"Jesus!" Schwartz's hand went for his gun.

"Hold it!"

The hand fell back limply; he knew he didn't have a chance.

The hired guns frisked Gross and Schwartz and relieved them of their hardware.

"Now face the wall," they were ordered.

Quickly and expertly the two steamer trunks were jimmied open with a crowbar and the suits and jackets were slit open. The bags of heroin were tucked away inside their overcoats. It was over in less than five minutes.

As they departed, the two paused at the doorway and took careful aim at Gross and Schwartz. Then six innocent sounding *pings*.

The Lepke men slid down the wall to the floor.

Minutes later Lepke and Gurrah arrived at the brownstone flat. With Gurrah scouting in front, they entered and walked down the dark hallway. Gurrah stiffened when he saw the half-open door. He waved Lepke back and, with gun drawn, he cautiously pushed the door open. The stark scene that greeted him neither surprised him nor moved him. Sooner or later it had been bound to happen.

He entered the room with Lepke following him. They walked past the rifled trunks to the two dead bodies on the floor. Stared down at them grimly, in silence.

Suddenly Gurrah's trained ear picked up alarming noises from outside in the street. Squealing tires as a car was gunned for a fast getaway. The engine roar frenized as it whipped past the house.

"Down!" He hurled Lepke and himself to the floor an instant before the machine-gun burst ripped through the thin walls of the building. On his hands and knees Gurrah crawled over to the window and returned the fire as the hit car sped away.

Lepke was shaken as he had never been shaken before. The world which until a few months ago had been his oyster was closing in on him.

Gurrah gave him a fond pat on the arm and said gruffly, "You know something? I think it's time you put on a disappearing act. You can't beat the anti-trust rap, and now Winchell's giving you too much bad publicity. You could use a little vacation, Lepke."

Lepke pressed his lips into a thin, grim line. "I think maybe I could."

The task of finding a safe hideout for Lepke was assigned to Abe "Kid Twist" Reles, a youthful, clean-cut young man who did not fit the popular image of a hood. It followed that he was a valuable go-between in sensitive jobs like this one.

The place Reles found was enough to offend the esthetic taste even of one as thick-skinned as Gurrah. It was a small storeroom behind the projection booth of a rundown movie theater.

Lepke was spirited to the theater by Gurrah and Reles, wearing a disguise that made him look like an Italian emigrant just getting off the boat.

He winced as he stooped to pass through the cramped doorway into a room that was even more cramped than his prison cell had been. A bare light bulb hung from the ceiling over a hard, narrow cot.

Gurrah was aghast. "Reles, is this the best you could do?"

Reles looked pained. "It's safe, and that's the important thing."

"Yeah," said Lepke dryly, testing the bed. "Ambassador Hotel, Miami Beach."

In the course of the next few weeks, Lepke saw more movies than he had seen during all of his life before. His favorites were the gangster flicks starring Cagney, Edward G. Robinson and molls that all looked like Jean Harlow.

Gurrah was with him a lot of the time, and together they would sit in the darkened theater eating sandwiches and drinking needle beer. Gurrah always took the epics on the screen very seriously and strongly disapproved of his boss's levity.

"What's so funny?" he growled one night.

"Those Hollywood shmucks. Do they really think gangsters act like that? What a cliche!"

"A what?"

"Never mind, dummy." He chuckled. "I ought to sue those guys."

"But the public, Lep, they love it. It's glamorous the way Hollywood does it."

When Lepke wanted to hold a mob meeting, the theater manager would simply put up a sign: SOLD

OUT or CLOSED FOR REPAIRS. Naturally the theater was a mob investment. As District Attorney Dewey increased the heat on Buchalter Enterprises, tighter security measures were required to keep Lepke out of the hands of the law.

At a crucial meeting attended by Gurrah, Reles and Rubin it was decided that the theater no longer was a safe hideout.

Rubin went over the company's books with Lepke and gave him the month's receipts in cash. It was a disappointing take.

"It's drying up," Lepke complained. "What the hell's going on, Max?"

Rubin shrugged. "You have to ask? Dewey. He's pressing us harder all the time."

Reles handed Lepke a "Wanted" poster with his photo on it.

"And he's put a price on your head, boss. It's all over town."

Lepke studied the poster with indignation. "Only twenty-four thousand? That's all he thinks I'm worth?"

"And you saved his life once, too," Gurrah said in an injured tone.

Lepke tapped the poster with a finger. "Is this place still safe?"

"We're gonna move you tonight," Reles assured him.

They took Lepke out of the theater after the evening performance disguised as a paraplegic in a wheelchair. Reles drove him to a modern apartment building in Flatbush, where arrangements had been made to hide him in the apartment of a mobster who had recently been killed in action.

The widow, Marion Waller, was a flashy blonde, and while no one had told her the real identity of her guest, Marion was not a dumb blonde. But she kept her mouth shut.

When Reles introduced Lepke as "Mr. Smith," she resisted the temptation to laugh.

"He's a good friend of your late husband," Reles told her.

Marion smiled. "Any friend of Fritzie's is a friend of mine. You're welcome here."

"Thank you, Mrs. Waller," Lepke said, eyeing her bosom.

She took charge of the wheelchair from Reles. "Let me take you to your room."

There was an old man who owned a newsstand on the corner with a good view of the apartment house entrance. He was being paid by Reles to keep a sharp lookout for lawmen. If anybody who looked like a cop entered the apartment, the old man was to duck down an alley, climb the fire escape and warn Lepke.

Meanwhile Thomas E. Dewey had been defeated in his bid for the office of New York's governor. Now he turned his undivided attention to his post as special prosecutor of vice and racketeering.

Robert Kane was a familiar visitor at Dewey's

office. They were in a very real sense friendly competitors, and both wanted Louis Lepke Buchalter. He was Number One on both the state's and federal government's most-wanted list.

Life for Lepke at the Waller apartment was far more pleasant than being cooped up in the little storeroom at the theater. There was one drawback as far as he was concerned. Mrs. Waller herself.

Every night when Lepke sat reading in his wheel-chair before bed, she would bring him in a cup of coffee or hot chocolate. Her flimsy negligees worn over even flimsier nightgowns left little doubt about her motive. Lepke pretended not to notice and maintained the pose of the crippled Mr. Smith, blind to her charms, always politely detached. He continued to address her as "Mrs. Waller."

One night Marion decided to alter her strategy. The coffee and cocoa had produced no results. She decided to switch to stronger medicine. After dinner that night she kept Lepke in the living room and persuaded him to have a few drinks with her. She wore a robe with nothing under it, and belted it loosely so that every time she moved or crossed her legs, he got an eyeful.

In spite of his undying loyalty to his beloved Bernice Lepke was a virile man, restless from being cooped up for so long, badly in need of some escape from his momentous worries and pressures, no matter how brief or how shallow. The drinks and Marion's sensuality began to weaken his resolve.

"Don't you miss your wife?" she asked him archly, crossing her leg wide and slow.

His hand trembled as he sipped his drink. "You know I do."

"Do I look something like her?"

He averted his face. "Nothing."

"How long's it been since you've seen her?"

"Too long."

They drank far into the night. Finally, Marion stood up and stretched, letting the negligee fall open. Lepke stared at her hungrily. In his drunken haze she was a montage of breasts and thighs and lips inviting him to a lusty feast.

"It's so goddamn hot," she yawned.

He shook his head. "Stop acting like a damned slut!"

She giggled and waved her fingers at him. "Well, time for bed, I think. Nighty-night and pleasant dreams."

Her mocking laughter trailed back to him as she went down the hall to her bedroom. Beads of sweat glistened on his forehead. The cords in his arms and along the backs of his hands stood out as he gripped the arms of the wheelchair with brute force. He squeezed his eyes shut, battling with every ounce of his will. But how much could a man take? *Christ!* he agonized. Surrendered at last. Slowly he rose from the wheelchair and staggered after her to the bedroom.

When he woke up the next morning, his head was

splitting. He lay there in the big double bed, staring at the ceiling, trying to get his thoughts back in focus. He had no recollection of the previous night. At first he thought he must be in his own bed back home. He listened to the sound of a shower running and in the background a radio was playing. Bernice always liked to play the radio when she was in the shower.

Gradually it came to him. This wasn't the bed he shared with his wife. His eyes wandered. No, this dump wasn't *his* bedroom!

It was like being struck by lightning when Marion emerged from the bathroom toweling her naked body, smiling. No, grinning like the cat that swallowed the canary!

He sat up, horrified.

'What's the matter with you, honey?" she asked, walking to the bed.

He pulled back from her. "Who are you?" Part of his mind was still numbed by alcohol.

Marion stared at him, unsure whether he was serious or joking. "Who am I? You've got to be kidding. You've only seen me every day for the past two months." She giggled. "You're a card, you are."

She went on rubbing the towel briskly over her belly and bottom, enjoying the sensual feel of the terry cloth. Remembering last night. She looked at Lepke with the sly grin of a conspirator.

"Say, you're okay—really something. You know, I was beginning to worry about you. I thought maybe *that* part of you *was* paralyzed. *Really* paralyzed."

With rising desire she knelt on the bed and ran her hands over his muscular body, tried to kiss him. "But I want to tell you something. That was really worth waiting for."

As her lips touched his cheek, Lepke went berserk. He picked her up bodily and flung her across the room as far as he could.

"You're filthy!" he screamed.

Dazed, she struggled up to a sitting position. "You crazy or something?"

He got out of the bed and wrapped a sheet around his body. "Do you think that if I weren't crazy from being cooped up in this rotten fleabag of yours that I'd go near a dirty used-up hole like yours?"

Crawling on all fours like a vicious wounded animal bent on wreaking vengeance on its tormentor, she went after him and grabbed the trailing sheet. She yanked it off him, screeching, "Look at that lily-white ass! Who do you think you are? The goddamned Prince of Wales?"

He whirled and slapped her hard on the side of the head, knocking her down again.

"Yeah, I'm the Prince of Wales and you're a goddamned whore!"

She got up and followed him to the bathroom door with the wet towel pressed against the side of her head where he'd hit her.

Her voice shook with hate and fury. "You can't talk to me that way. You can't slap me around! I don't give a damn who you might be—*Mr. Buchalter!* Yeah, that's right! Mr. Lepke Bullshitter! You think I ever believed that Mr. Smith crap?"

She took a robe off the back of the door and put it on. Lepke stood at the sink, washing, his back to her.

Marion continued her tirade. "I knew who you were the minute I set eyes on you! You didn't fool me with that wheelchair. Jesus! The likes of *you* moralizing to me! You've been drooling over me ever since you got here—watching me, following me with your eyes, practically undressing me! *You*—holding up that wife of yours like she's the Virgin Mary! What kind of a woman would marry a murderer like you?"

She realized too late that she had gone too far. With a cold, methodical deliberation that was more menacing than a show of temper, he turned off the water and turned to face her very slowly. The look in his eyes paralyzed her with fear.

"Get out of here, you hear me?" he said very quietly.

Her voice rose in hysteria. "*You* get out. This is my apartment. Anybody's gonna leave, it's gonna be you!"

She backed off slowly as he came toward her. "No! You stay away from me!"

He trapped her against the bed and hit her open-handed, one hand and then the other, so that her head flew back and forth like a punching bag.

He threw her away from him like a rag doll. He didn't want to touch her with his bare hands and defile himself any more. With murderous intent he looked around for something to hit her with. He wanted to kill her. He told her:

"Get out of here, you dirty slut, or I'll kill you!"

Marion knew in her bones that he meant it. She scrambled wildly for the door as he picked up a clock off the bed table and hurled it at her head. She ducked and it smashed against the wall. The girl fled for her life down the hall.

The rage drained out of him slowly, leaving him weak and trembling. He sank down on the bed and buried his face in his hands.

The radio on the shelf outside the bathroom was still playing, a lively melody:

"... *every evening ... every morning ... ain't we got fun. ...*"

Chapter
Thirteen

That afternoon Marion Waller walked into the police station and demanded to see "the man in charge of dope pushers."

The desk sergeant was understandably confused. "Slow down, lady, slow down. I can't make head or tail out of what you're saying. You wanna see *who?*"

Marion put a hand on her hip. "I don't *know* who I want to see. Just somebody who's in charge of dope and dope pushers and dope smugglers and stuff like that!"

"Okay, okay—but tell me what's your problem. Start from the beginning."

Marion began with the night Reles had brought "Mr. Smith" to her apartment in a wheelchair.

When she was finished, the sergeant conferred with his captain, and they decided that this was a matter for the federal agents who had been snooping around New York for weeks. Marion was taken to Robert

Kane's office, where she told her story to Kane and his partner Elson.

As she went through an elaborate description of the Buchalter mob's recent activities, Elson interrupted her: "And how do you know all this?"

Marion snorted. "He's been living in my apartment for over two months. I've got ears. His boys visit, they talk about dope. My walls are paper thin and I heard, you can bet I heard."

"And you'd be willing to testify to all of this in court?" Kane inquired.

"Just try me."

Kane picked up a pencil and pad. "Where is your apartment?"

Within the hour New York police and federal agents were closing in on Lepke. The old man who owned the newspaper stand saw the caravan approaching far down the block. Following instructions, he ran back down the alleyway and climbed the fire escape to warn Lepke.

When the lawmen broke into the Waller apartment, the radio was on and a cup of coffee was steaming on the kitchen table. But Louis Lepke Buchalter had vanished.

Ironically, the radio was tuned in on Walter Winchell's newscast. Robert Kane listened to it with a sense of bitter frustration:

". . . on this sizzling July 10, 1939, the race to bring fugitive racketeer Louis "Lepke" Buchalter to justice is keeping New York's finest *pretty* busy. . . . The phone calls are backed up on the switchboard at police headquarters. *Everybody* has a lead to Lepke's whereabouts. They have leads on a bearded Lepke, a bald Lepke, a mustachioed Lepke; even a Lepke with horns has been reported. . . . There is a unique rivalry in the contest to hunt down Lepke. J. Edgar Hoover's F.B.I. agents want him on narcotic charges, and the New York State District Attorney, Tom Dewey, has enough evidence to put him away for five hundred years. . . . Mr. Dewey, capturing Lepke wouldn't hurt your political fortunes—"

Kane snapped off the radio and grimaced at Elson. "I hope they don't get him before we do."

So determined was J. Edgar Hoover his F.B.I. should capture Lepke that he came up to New York to conduct the hunt personally.

"We're declaring war on the entire underworld until Lepke is in our hands," he told Kane. "I want every hood who's ever known Lepke subpoenaed to testify before the grand jury."

It was a brilliant strategy. For years there has always been a tacit understanding between the criminal world and law enforcement agencies that the law will close its eyes to certain illegal activities, if for no other reason than it is more practical to concentrate on the more serious offenses. There are not enough men, not enough money, not enough time, not enough space on the courts' dockets to prosecute every hood who makes book or sells a case of bootleg whiskey.

Now Hoover declared that kind of amnesty null and void. When the first batch of underworld figures were ordered to appear in court, they were indifferent. Word was out that Hoover wanted Lepke handed over, but there was no way he could strong-arm them, they believed. All they had to do on the witness stand was to admit they knew him: *"Yes, I know Mr. Buchalter, but I haven't seen him in months."* And they would be off the hook.

Only it didn't work that way. Abner "Longy" Zwillman, chief of Lepke's New Jersey mob, was the first witness called before the grand jury. To his shock, he was not even questioned about Lepke. Instead the U.S. Attorney conducted an incisive, probing, interrogation about Longy's activities going back to Prohibition, matters he had believed were long ago swept under the rug.

To answer the questions, he would have had to implicate himself and other associates in a variety of nefarious crimes, including income tax evasion. On advice of his lawyer, he refused to answer.

In those days the Fifth Amendment did not have the support from our courts that it enjoys today.

The presiding judge gave him six months in prison for contempt of court.

That was only the beginning of the parade. Hoover

let the word spread throughout the criminal community that he was going to send a hundred and fifty key mob leaders to jail unless the F.B.I. got Lepke.

After the first half-dozen hoods were busted for contempt and sent up for six months, the Board of Directors held an emergency meeting presided over by Lucky Luciano. By unanimous vote it was decided that Lepke should appear before the august body and state his case—if any.

The message was delivered by Kid Twist Reles to Lepke, now hiding out in a dingy Brooklyn hotel. He read the letter while Gurrah looked on anxiously.

"What is it, Lep?"

"The Syndicate wants to see me."

"You're not going?"

Lepke's mouth curled arrogantly. "Got no choice. You know the rules. Look, there's one thing I have to do before I go there. I want to see Bernice and the boy."

Gurrah's head hung. "Sure, Lep." This was the beginning of the end; he could feel it in his bones.

He picked up Bernice at her apartment. As he had instructed her, she was disguised in slacks, turban and dark glasses. The moment he pulled away from the curb, he spotted the car tailing them.

"Hang on, Bernice," he told her grimly. "This is going to be a rough ride."

Gurrah was an old pro at this game, and he led the tail car a wild, frantic chase through the narrow streets of East New York. When there was no sign of the other car in the rear-view mirror for ten minutes, Gurrah breathed easy.

"We lost 'em," he told Bernice with satisfaction. "Now we go to Yeshiva."

David was waiting for them out front of the school. He ran to the car and got in quickly. Gurrah gunned the engine and they sped off. He took no notice of the small, battered sedan parked across the street from Yeshiva. It was facing the other way and appeared to be empty.

He did not see the three heads pop up off the floor of the car as soon as the big Rolls had taken off.

They were supposed to meet Lepke in an abandoned amusement park. Bernice had always loved to take David to Coney Island when he was younger. There was a lighthearted gaiety about the gaudy color and hurdy-gurdy music, the whirling merry-go-rounds and the screams and laughter of happy children.

But there was nothing happy about this deserted place. A ghost town. The still ponies on the carousel with their wild eyes had a menacing air about them. The gargantuan clown painted over the entrance to the fun house was fiendish looking. And the deathly silence. Bernice shivered and pulled David closer to her as they followed Gurrah to a building on one side of the grounds.

They entered an eerie, dim world that was more frightening than the one outside. It was a storehouse for broken-down equipment, a graveyard of amusement park castoffs.

But the coldness dissipated within her when she was in her husband's arms for the first time in months.

Self-conscious about intruding on the family reunion, Gurrah went back to the door and looked out. He cursed softly to himself. The battered car that had been parked across from David's school was pulling through the park gate.

"Lep!" he said with an urgency that brought Lepke hurrying over.

"What is it?"

Gurrah opened the door a crack. "Take a look."

"You let 'em tail you," Lepke said reprovingly.

Gurrah was confused. "I don't know how. I lost the first tail, I know I did. But they must of had another waiting for me at Yeshiva. Look, you and Bernice and the kid duck out the back door."

"What'll you do?"

"Don't worry about me." He patted his gun. "I'll see you later."

There was no lock on the door, so Gurrah braced himself against it while Lepke and his family went out the rear door. He bought them time as the three men outside hurled their combined weights against the door. Gurrah was big and strong, but eventually he was overcome by sheer numbers. They broke in and Gurrah went sprawling.

Two of them began searching for Lepke inside

the cluttered building, while the third man ran to the back door. He flung it open and saw the three running figures.

"I got him!" he shouted and drew his gun.

"Like hell!" Gurrah pulled out his gun and dropped him before he could squeeze off a shot.

The gunfire brought the other two running at him from opposite directions, blasting Gurrah with their weapons. He fell to his knees, but managed to fire two more shots before they dropped him permanently with another volley. The force of the slugs knocked him flat on his back. Before his eyes closed forever, Gurrah saw that he had hit one of the remaining two.

The last man, ignoring Gurrah and his fallen companions, set out after Lepke, who was circling around the park on a circuitous route back to the car.

He halted at the sound of the gunfire and looked back in the direction of the building.

"Gurrah needs help," he said.

"No, Louis!" Bernice was terrified.

He looked around for a suitable hiding place for his wife and son, spotted a dark crawl space under the Whirl-a-Way ride.

"Get under there. I'm going back!"

She grabbed him, pleading, "No, Louis! Please."

He removed her hands gently but firmly. "I'm going back."

Bernice was paralyzed with fear.

"Goddamit! Do what I say!" he shouted. He put

a hand on David's arm. "Take your mother, David. You're going to be the man of the house while I'm away."

When they were safely concealed, he took out his gun and headed back to the building. He slipped in through the back-door. Stood pressed against the wall while his eyes became accustomed to the dimness. It was deathly silent.

He walked heavily past the bodies of the two strangers to where his old friend lay. Gurrah looked so peaceful, almost as if he were asleep. He dropped to his knees beside the body, observing a moment of silence. Then with a sigh he touched his cheek and stood up.

He was void of all emotion, anger, grief, fear. There would be time to feel later. At the moment all of his energy and concentration had to be conserved for one thing. Destroying the third man!

He went back to the door and peered out into the brilliant sunlight, squinting as his eyes scanned the landscape. He saw nothing. There were innumerable places to hide in an amusement park, like the place where he had left Bernice and David.

Alert as an Indian scout, he started back to find his wife and son with the gun held ready. By the time he reached the Whirl-a-Way, he was starting to relax. Maybe, he thought, the other man had cut out after his friends were killed.

That untypical kind of positive thinking almost cost him dearly. As he, Bernice and David walked

135

back to the car, the third gunman jumped up on the platform of the nearby merry-go-round and stalked them, moving from one horse to another, seeking a clear shot at Lepke.

He got his chance as they approached the car. Bracing his arm on the back of a stationary horse, he took careful aim and fired. The shot whizzed past Lepke's ear.

"Get into the car!" Lepke shouted and whirled to return the fire. His shot sent up splinters from the horse into the gunman's face, spoiling his aim. His shot was wild, and Lepke sprinted across the grass to the cover of the carousel's control booth.

They exchanged another round of shots, but the position was pretty much of a stalemate, Lepke judged. Neither one could take the initiative without exposing himself to the other's fire. Unless.. . . . Lepke's gaze swept across the interior of the control booth. Fixed on the main switch. Purposefully he reached inside and pulled it.

With a lazy rumble and roar the mechanism shuddered to life. Music blared out of the loud speakers. The shock of finding the carousel suddenly moving, with the distraction of the horses pumping up and down, totally demoralized the gunman. Too late he realized that the revolving platform was taking him right into Lepke's line of fire. As he came abreast of the control booth, he squeezed off one last desperate shot.

Aiming coolly and carefully, Lepke put his shot

squarely in his enemy's heart. The man slumped forward across the horse's saddle.

With dark humor Lepke was reminded of the western movies he had seen when he was hiding out in the theater.

The villain's dead body was always carried back to town, slung across the saddle of his horse!

He pocketed the gun and walked back to the Rolls-Royce.

Chapter
Fourteen

On the day of his hearing before the Syndicate board members, Lepke arrived in style at Luciano's Royal Hotel headquarters in his Rolls—fashionably late. He got out, straightened his silk tie, pulled down the jacket of his Palm Beach jacket and threw a haughty glance at the hoods guarding the main entrance.

In the foyer of Luciano's suite he was relieved of his gun, which was placed on a rack along with a dozen or so other holstered weapons. It was a scorching hot day, and he hung his jacket up before going into the meeting room.

It was as rich and tastefully appointed as the board room of any bank or corporation. Luciano was a vain man personally and professionally.

Lepke greeted the other bosses with a nod and a nickname. Luciano, at the head of the table with Anastasia at his right, scowled when Lepke addressed him as "Lucky." As he mellowed and got richer and more influential, he had come to despise its cheap connotation.

Lepke took his place with a sneer. "This is a switch. The Judge being judged."

Luciano was as tactful as possible. "Ever since you've been a lammister, business has been terrible. You know what's been happening; Hoover has declared war against us. At the rate things have been going, all of us will be in stir before long unless. . . ." He let it hang.

"I know, Charley," he said bitterly.

"No use getting sore, Lepke. It's nothing personal. We all like and respect you—you know that." Luciano's smirk said something quite different. "But no one guy is bigger than the organization. That's the way it is; that's the way it's always gonna be."

Lepke was impassive. "So, what's the verdict? You gonna mix me up with cement and drop me in the river?"

Luciano feigned dismay. "No! No, Lepke! The way we see it"—he indicated the board members seated around the table—"you got a choice. Turn yourself in to the feds or to the D.A. It's up to you."

"Thanks for nothing. I'll take the feds."

Luciano shrugged and smiled. "We'll miss you, Lepke."

Lepke stood up slowly, staring contemptuously at the vice and dope king. Like you miss Gurrah. You're a liar . . . Lucky!"

As Lepke walked slowly along the table toward him, Luciano rose stiffly. The two men stood eyeball to eyeball for a moment of silence that seemed an eternity to the other nervous mobsters at the table.

A gasp went up as Lepke whipped one hand back and forth across Luciano's cheeks. Luciano winced, but his arms remained rigid at his sides.

In cold fury, Lepke backhanded him with his right as hard as he could. Luciano reeled back and held on to the back of his chair for support. The other mobsters began to push back their chairs, ready to duck under the table or make a break for the door.

Lepke smiled and spread out his arms like wings. "All right, Lucky—now kill *me*."

Luciano straightened up, took a handkerchief and dabbed at the trickle of blood on the left side of his mouth. He smiled back at Lepke. The hate generated between these two was a palpable force in the room that stifled the other men.

Luciano's voice rasped. "I should kill you, but the organization needs you to get the heat off. You'll die in stir, nice and slow. Nice and slow—I'll enjoy that, Lepke, I'll really enjoy it."

Lepke's gaze did not waver. "All right, so I'll turn myself in. I'll need a few days to negotiate with the feds."

Luciano looked to Anastasia. "Fair enough. But until then my boys will help your boys take care of you."

Lepke's last days of freedom were spent in an abominable basement room located underneath the Brooklyn Bridge.

Anastasia, with a squad of Luciano hoods, occupied the ground floor. One or more of Lepke's hoods guarded him. As time went on, he was less and less certain of the connotation of the word "guarded."

Playing solitaire on his narrow daybed, Lepke watched Kid Twist posted at the doorway. His hand moved reflexively to his gun every time Lepke got up to go to the john or get a drink of water.

The anxiety of the past few days was taking its toll on him. Unshaven, unkempt and unwashed, he felt like an untouchable. His hand trembled when he shuffled the cards.

For some quixotic reason, Lepke had chosen columnist Walter Winchell to act as the go-between for him and the F.B.I. He had always entertained a healthy respect for the newsman's toughness, style and outspokenness, even when Winchell was reviling him and the Syndicate as no other reporter had ever dared to do.

At last the negotiations were coming to a conclusion. One morning there was a knock from the room above. Lepke leapt up and went to the dumbwaiter shaft.

Anastasia's voice megaphoned down to him hollowly. "He's here."

141

Lepke whirled to Reles, motioning to the table, littered with dirty dishes, ashtrays and glasses.

"Hey, Kid, clean the shit." He called up to Anastasia. "Tell him to give me a minute."

Lepke put on his jacket and tie and combed his hair. He looked like a bum in the rumpled clothes and he knew it. He ran a hand over the stubble on his face with distaste. Folding his hands behind him, he composed himself and waited.

Minutes later Anastasia came into the basement room preceded by an erect, distinguished-looking man whom he recognized immediately as Winchell.

Anastasia cleared his throat with self-importance. "Mr. Buchalter, Mr. Winchell is here to see you."

Striving for the right degree of arrogance, Lepke said, "Ah, the great Mr. Winchell! The voice of the twentieth century."

"Thank you," Winchell said, one eyebrow lifting superciliously. The voice was less urgent than it was on radio.

Lepke nodded to Reles, who stood off to one side tensely, hand on gun. "Kid, our best cognac for Mr. Winchell." He looked the newsman up and down. "You know, I'd figured you'd be taller."

Winchell's mouth twitched, but he managed to suppress a smile. He accepted the drink of dark-looking booze that Lepke handed him with a nod.

"Well, can we drink to the deal you made?" Lepke asked, trying to cover his nervousness with casualness. A yawn. Flicking lint off his sleeve.

"It's set for tomorrow," Winchell told him.

"How about Dewey?"

"Hoover gave his word he won't turn you over to New York."

"I never trust a cop," Reles observed.

"*Shut up!*" Lepke snapped with some of his old authority. "How many years?"

"Twelve—at the most."

He could not hide his relief. "Twelve. . . ." He managed to get the glass to his mouth without spilling it and gulped down the mind-numbing whiskey.

That night they brought Bernice to visit him. When she arrived Lepke was sleeping fitfully on the hard bed. The bedclothes were drenched with sweat.

He sat up in a daze when the light exploded in the darkness, and shielded his eyes. "Whoosit?"

"You sent for me?" the dark figure standing at the foot of the bed said. He recognized his wife's voice.

"I can't see you in this light."

She switched off the naked lamp bulb on the table beside the bed.

He motioned to her. "Come here."

Moving stiffly, she came to his side. Her hands were folded primly in front of her, and when he touched her arm, it was cold and unresponsive. He squeezed her hand. It was as limp as a dead fish.

Frowning, he looked into her face. "You're trembling. Do you feel all right?"

She nodded mutely.

"Sit down." He tugged at her hand, but she held back.

His voice was gentle. "Sit down—please."

There was a long pause, and when she did speak, her voice was choked and wavering. "No. . . . No, Louis, I—I shouldn't have come."

Her words twisted a knife in his heart. "Why did you?" he asked lifelessly.

"I—I—" She averted her face from him. "I'd better go."

He let her hand slip away from him and told her, "Then go."

Chapter
Fifteen

The following night Lepke was driven to his rendezvous with the F.B.I. in a mob limousine. At precisely ten o'clock he was dropped off at the corner of Fifth Avenue and 28th Street in New York. He crossed the street to another car parked on the opposite curb. Two men were sitting in the front seat.

Without hesitation, Lepke opened the back door and got in. The driver turned to him.

"Hello, Louis." It was Robert Kane.

"Hello, Robert."

Winchell was the other man.

Lepke frowned. "The condition was that *he* would be here personally."

"That's right." Kane motioned to a figure slipping out of the shadows of a store front. A short, stocky man with a bulldog face. He was scowling when he got into the car. Thugs like Lepke didn't issue ultimatums and hand down conditions to the chief of the Federal Bureau of Investigation. It was probably the one time in his life that J. Edgar Hoover had let anyone but himself call the shots. Friend or foe.

"Mr. Hoover, this is Lepke," Winchell introduced them.

Hoover glared at him with undisguised scorn.

"Twelve years, that's what we agreed?" Lepke got right down to business.

Hoover and Winchell exchanged a look that said more than his pronouncement:

"That will be up to the judge."

Kane whirled around in the front seat and stared at his chief in shock. He started to speak, but Lepke spoke first.

Quietly, without emotion, almost with relief. The ordeal was over at last. And when it came down to the hard, cold facts, he knew he had no right to expect anything else. He and Hoover had a lot in common. They both played the game for keeps. No quarter. No mercy.

"What are we waiting for?" Lepke snapped. "The sooner I get there, the sooner I get out." He closed his eyes and leaned back on the seat.

Lepke received no quarter from the courts either. He was sentenced to twelve years for conspiracy to violate the narcotics laws, an additional two years on the antitrust indictments. After serving his term, he was to be transferred from Leavenworth Penitentiary and handed over to the state of New York.

A triumphant Dewey sat in the front row of the courtroom when the sentence was handed down. A bitter Robert Kane was there too; he refused to look at or talk to J. Edgar Hoover. Afterward, he drove grief-stricken Bernice back to her apartment.

"It's not over yet, Bernice," he tried to comfort her. "There are appeals."

She shook her head. "Give up, already—you've done your best."

"It's the first time I've heard *you* giving up."

She sighed. "He'll be in prison for the rest of his life. Maybe that's better." She read the look of silent disapproval in his face and explained. "Bobby, don't look at me like that. I loved him. When he was with me, I shut my eyes to everything else."

She could not hold back the tears any longer. "Oh, Bobby, I do love him!"

He put his arms around her and held her tightly until the wracking sobs stopped and she hung limp in his embrace.

Louis "Lepke" Buchalter served only two years in Leavenworth before he was turned over to prosecutor Thomas Dewey in New York. When he met with his attorney for the first time in the detention room of the prison, counselor Glass was shocked by his appearance. He was gray, wan and thin; he had aged ten years in two. But the bulldog tenacity had not deserted him.

"I'm gonna beat this rap, Arnold," he maintained.

"So what have they got? They got nothing. Absolutely nothing!"

"There's Allie Tannenbaum—and there's also Max Rubin," Glass reminded him.

Lepke scoffed at the idea. "My Max? Max wouldn't—he wouldn't talk to the D.A. Max would never do a thing like that. Not to me."

"I'm sorry, Louis," Glass said quietly. "Max has already agreed to testify against you. He'll tell everything he knows."

Lepke was stunned. "Why?"

"To save his own skin, Louis. Things have changed since you've been away. Even politicians can't be bought anymore; not as easily as in the old days anyway."

Lepke's eyes narrowed, and for a moment that old look was there, the steely menace that could wither a man almost as effectively as if he were staring down a gun barrel.

"How old is Max?"

"Forty-eight."

Lepke clasped his hands together decisively. "That's a ripe old age."

Not long after that, Max Rubin was returning to his home one evening accompanied by his wife and daughter, when two men emerged from a dark doorway and grabbed Rubin. While the wife and daughter looked on in terror, the mob's top executioner, Mendy, pressed a revolver to the base of his skull and fired one shot. Rubin fell to the sidewalk, and they made their escape as the girl screamed for help and her mother fainted.

The next day Allie Tannenbaum was coming out of his favorite delicatessen when two gunmen came up in back of him and ordered him to get into a long, black limousine parked at the curb.

Tannenbaum figured his number was up. "Please don't kill me," he begged.

The car door swung open, and to his amazement, he was looking into the smiling face of Lucky Luciano.

"Nobody's going to kill you, Allie," Luciano assured him. "Over my dead body, my friend."

Luciano's gang held Tannenbaum in "protective custody" until it was his turn to testify at Lepke's murder trial.

Dewey wasted no time when he got him on the witness stand.

"When Lepke wanted someone eliminated, did he usually give the order personally?"

"No, sir. It was Gurrah Shapiro gave 'em. He always gave 'em, except that day."

"And what was Mr. Lepke's mood on the Friday before Mr. Rosen's murder?"

"Oh, he was boiling. I never seen him so mad."

"What about?"

"He was screaming over and over again: 'Rosen's making deals with Dewey.'"

A stir went through the spectators in the packed courtroom.

Dewey leaned closer to the witness. "What did Lepke say then?"

Tannenbaum took a long breath and let it out with a nervous glance at the defense table where Lepke sat glowering at him.

He gulped. "He said, 'I want Rosen hit. I want that sonofabitch dead!'"

Lepke whispered to Glass. "You gonna let him get away with that?"

"Take it easy," Glass quieted him. "It's his word against yours."

Dewey proceded: "Now, Mr. Tannenbaum, will you tell the court—was there anybody else in the room who could have heard Lepke say what you claim he said?"

Tannenbaum rubbed his chin. "Like I said, there was Gurrah Shapiro. Yeah, and there was Mr. Rubin. Both dead now. No one else."

Dewey turned away abruptly. "You're excused, Mr. Tannenbaum."

Glass cupped a hand to Lepke's ear. "They can't make Tannenbaum's testimony hold up without a corroborating witness."

Lepke settled back smugly as the judge asked the D.A., "Is this the last witness for the prosecution, Mr. Dewey?"

Dewey looked even smugger than Lepke. "No, Your Honor. We have one more witness. With your permission I would like to call him now."

There was a murmur of anticipation from the

spectators. The atmosphere was charged; they could sense that something momentous was about to take place.

"Let's proceed," the Judge said, feeling it himself.

Dewey's voice crackled as he pronounced, "I want to call Mr. Max Rubin to the witness stand."

The judge called for order as the people began to babble excitedly, and all eyes turned toward the entrance to the courtroom.

He addressed the prosecutor sharply. "Mr. Dewey, are you calling spirits into this courtroom?"

Dewey allowed himself a smile. "No, Your Honor. Mr. Max Rubin is very much alive. I now call him to the stand."

The doors swung open at the rear of the room and an attendant pushed a wheelchair down the aisle. Rubin sat rigidly in the chair, gripping the arms tensely. His head was swathed in bandages. His face was pale and wan. His glazed eyes radiated the sick fear of an animal in a steel trap.

The wheelchair was placed alongside the witness stand and Dewey began his examination.

"We don't want to keep you too long, Mr. Rubin. Can you tell the court one thing? Did you hear Louis Buchalter, Lepke as you know him, order the murder of Joseph Rosen?"

Rubin nodded his head and opened his mouth but nothing came out.

"We can't hear you," Dewey said.

Rubin swallowed and this time, it rang out loud

and clear. "Yes. He said, 'I want Rosen hit. I want the sonofabitch dead!' "

Lepke slumped down in his chair at the defense table. He met Dewey's smile of victory with stony indifference. Already he was dead inside. The rest of it was purely a formality.

Chapter
Sixteen

The personal vendetta between Thomas E. Dewey and Louis "Lepke" Buchalter was still not finished, though.

In 1942 Dewey was swept into office as governor of New York State on the strength of his brilliant achievements as the racket-busting district attorney who nailed Lepke and scores of other mobsters and racketeers.

As governor it was within his powers to commute Lepke's death sentence, but he adamantly refused to show clemency. Even a personal appeal from his old friend and associate Robert Kane did not move him.

"I'm sorry, Bob," he said. "This sentence is long overdue. I won't postpone it any longer. I have a responsibility to the people of New York."

Kane's contention was that there was more involved in the issue than the execution of Lepke.

The very nature of capital punishment was on trial, and he was firmly opposed to it.

"But Tom, how can you play politics with human life?" he demanded at one point in their discussion.

Dewey was indignant. "Politics? This man has killed over sixty people."

"And if the state kills him, there'll be one more victim."

The governor sighed and there was genuine sympathy for Kane in his voice. "You're a lawyer, Bob, a man of law and order. You're not seriously suggesting that we abolish capital punishment in New York?"

"I'm not suggesting it. I am saying that it will come to pass. If not in your term of office, then under the next governor. Or maybe the one after him. But it will be, Tom, you'll see. One day capital punishment will be abolished everywhere in this country."

Kane told Lepke the bad news himself on the day of his execution. He arrived as Lepke was in the midst of the traditional last meal.

As a man who had indulged all of his lusty appetites in life, the prospect of death was not about to inhibit him. When Kane walked into his cell, he was attacking a table laden with delicacies in the style of a true gourmet.

Licking a finger, he grinned at Kane. "Why, counselor."

"The warden gave me special permission to see you," was the grim reply.

"Good, good. Want to join me?"

Kane stood before him silently.

"Come on," Lepke urged, "it's Saturday night."

He spit it out. "Louis, we've been turned down."

Lepke did not interrupt the rhythm of his chewing. "That sonofabitch—and to think I once saved his life." He shook his head, deploring the thanklessness of life.

"Louis, I've failed you," Kane said in anguish.

"Failed me? Why? I mean, you got me an extra two years on appeals. Come on." He poured a drink for Kane and handed it to him.

Kane ignored it. He stared at the table, thinking of *the* Last Supper. "Somehow, I—I"

"Cut that out. This is supposed to be a party." He slugged down the drink himself and wiped his mouth. With the impish humor that Kane had always found appealing about the man, he joked, "Hey, listen, are you sure we can't buy Dewey?"

A weak smile flickered across Kane's face.

The guard at the door called their attention to the rabbi waiting quietly in the shadows to bestow the final blessing on Lepke before he took leave of this world.

Lepke was curiously attentive to the rites of the death house, almost as if he were a spectator at his own execution. Detached and unemotional.

First the bath. Donning the loose white sack shirt

and the loose dark pants with the leg slit. Leg and head shaved for the electrodes. White socks and slippers. A comfortable outfit to wear for a stroll along Miami Beach.

Walking the "last mile" down the corridor to the little green door.

Inside the little "theater," the electric chair up front and four rows of benches for the audience. He gave a cursory glance at the blur of faces, newsmen and witnesses, picked out Robert Kane. Kane looked like he was the one going to die. Lepke felt sorry for him. He shook off the guards' hands defiantly and walked to the chair with a firm step. He sat down, nodded to the rabbi at his side reading from his prayer book.

Robert Kane wanted to close his eyes to the grisly drama, but some intangible force kept his eyes riveted on Lepke.

Two attendants stepped forward and strapped the restraining belts about his body. Stooped to fasten the electrodes to his legs. Lepke glanced up idly as the big electrode was lowered onto his shaved scalp.

Kane shuddered as the electricity charged through Lepke, causing his arms and legs to twitch and vibrate. His slippers were flung off, and where the electrode was fixed to his right leg, Kane saw the flesh char, like steak grilling over charcoal. The sweet, pungent odor of cooking flesh.

At last he could shut his eyes.

When it was over, Kane left the prison and walked to a small park about a block away, where Bernice and David were waiting.

He put his hand on her shoulder. "It's done," he said. "His troubles are over and he's at peace."

She rose slowly, and with David on one side and Kane on the other, walked off into the night.

Soon it would be dawn, and Bernice would take Louis home with her.

CANADIAN Paperback Originals by Canadian Authors

FICTION

☐ **THE LOVELIEST AND THE BEST by Angela O'Connell.** An adult love story for the men and women who lived World War II . . (78621—$1.50)

☐ **BACKROOM BOYS AND GIRLS by John Philip Maclean.** A novel that raises basic questions about Canadian politicians—and sex. (78622—$1.50)

☐ **THE QUEERS OF NEW YORK by Leo Orenstein.** A novel of the homosexual underworld. ....(78262—$1.25)

☐ **RIGHT NOW WOULD BE A GOOD TIME TO CUT MY THROAT by Paul Fulford.** A bawdy sailor adrift in Toronto publishing circles. (78252—$1.25)

☐ **FESTIVAL by Bryan Hay.** A modern novel which reveals the rip-off of drug-crazy kids by music festival promoters ....(77536—.95)

☐ **THE GHOSTS OF WAR by Michael Foxwell.** A love story which reveals the after-effects of war. ....(78644—$1.50)

☐ **GOD AND MRS. SULLIVAN—Joy Carroll.** The love affairs of a beautiful society woman with too much money .....(78658—$1.50)

☐ **DADDY'S DARLING DAUGHTER—William Thomas.** A shocking novel of today's children and their life-style ....(78740—$1.50)

☐ **WILD INHERITANCE—Robert Thurman.** The gripping story of one family's struggle for survival—and success ....(78738—$1.50)

☐ **LOVE AFFAIR—Earl Knickerbocker.** The bitter-sweet romance of two young schoolteachers. ....(78744—$1.50)

☐ **THE LAST CANADIAN—William Heine.** A terrifying look at the future. (78743—$1.50)

SIMON & SCHUSTER of Canada Ltd.
330 Steelcase Road, Markham, Ontario

Please send me the POCKET BOOKS I have checked above. I am enclosing $.................(check or money order—no currency or C.O.D.'s. Please include the list price plus 25 cents to cover handling and mailing costs.)

Name ....

Address ....

City .... Province .... Zone ....

C01/73

CANADIAN
Paperback Originals
by Canadian Authors

NONFICTION

☐ **WHY WEAR GLASSES?** by Dr. B. J. Slatt & Dr. H. A. Stein. A layman's guide to eye problems and the new soft contact lens.
(78565—$2.50)

☐ **THE SUMMER OLYMPIC GAMES** by Jock Carroll. Did you know Canada has won more than 250 medals in the Summer Olympics? A complete guide to the games & records. 100 photos of champions in action, with special attention to Canadian athletes. (78569—$2.50)

☐ **Crosbie's DICTIONARY OF PUNS** by John Crosbie. The world's punniest book and the world's first pun dictionary. .. (78217—$1.25)

☐ **PRO HOCKEY 74-75**—Jim Proudfoot. The hockey fan's annual Bible, by the Sports Editor of The Toronto Star .... (78750—$1.95)

☐ **Percy Rowe's TRAVEL GUIDE TO CANADA.** The first complete guide to every province & territory. Hotels, restaurants, museums, parks, campsites. .... (78596—$1.50)

☐ **SOME CANADIAN GHOSTS** by Sheila Hervey. An examination of strange occurrences and appearances across Canada. (78629—$1.50)

☐ **ALL QUIET ON THE RUSSIAN FRONT** by Kurt Stock. A German soldier, now a Canadian, reveals the horror of Russian P.O.W. camps.
(78630—$1.50)

☐ **THE HAPPY HAIRDRESSER** by Nicholas Loupos. A rollicking revelation of what Canadian women do and say when they let their hair down. .... (78654—$1.50)

☐ **DOWN THE ROAD**—Jock Carroll. Uninhibited talks with Marilyn Monroe and other famous sex symbols. Photos ..... (78739—$1.50)

C02/73

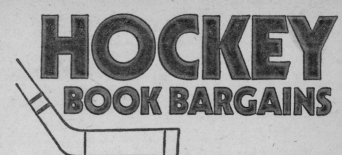

HOCKEY BOOK BARGAINS